❧BLOSSOM CREEK SERIES❧

# BLOSSOM CREEK

*NY TIMES & USA TODAY BESTSELLING AUTHOR*

# LEXI BUCHANAN

# A RAKE IN BLOSSOM CREEK
BLURB

Not looking for any more complications in his life, especially of the female variety, Ryker De La Fuente visits family in Blossom Creek. He's hoping the change of scenery will ease his mind and help him focus on the decision he needs to make in Italy. However, before he arrives in Blossom Creek, his plans derail when he drives the town's own, Beatrice Leonard, off the road during a snowstorm.

Beatrice is different in a refreshing way, and he finds his interest piqued, which confuses him. The one thing Ryker shouldn't be doing in Blossom Creek is flirting with an attractive woman who makes his blood warm when he's only visiting. He can't resist the shy beauty, and of course, one thing leads to another, giving the town something new to gossip about.

While Ryker is preoccupied with Beatrice, the newly formed ladies' Book Club finds the new fire chief to be an intriguing topic of discussion.

# A RAKE IN BLOSSOM CREEK

## PROLOGUE - RYKER

SNOW.

Heavy snow falls from the sky as I drive toward Blossom Creek. Tomorrow night is the opening of my cousin's restaurant, Emelia's. I haven't let anyone know that I'm going to be in town because I hadn't wanted to disappoint Levi and Emma if I changed my mind.

My life is messed up, and I need time to think, which I can't do in Italy. So, I'd gotten on a plane and flew home to my family. Well, part of my family. My parents and two sisters are home in Great Falls, which is where I'll be heading eventually.

Visibility becomes more dangerous, and the thought crosses my mind that I might be safer parking the car and walking. Then again, the road is narrow and knowing my luck, I'd probably get hit by a car. Town is up ahead, maybe five minutes. I grip the steering wheel in determination. Having grown up with heavy snow in the winter months, I've come to dislike it, but I'm used to it. I can drive in it. Nothing was easy when the snow arrived in Montana, which is why I had escaped to the sunshine of Europe as soon as I was old enough. California would have been closer, but I had the same itch as my father once had—fast cars, fast women, and of course, the urge to travel.

The wipers are noisy as they swish back and forth on the highest setting, yet their attempt at clearing the window is futile.

Chevrons appear in my headlights, warning of a sharp bend in the road to the left. I swallow around the slither of fear racing through me and take the curve slowly only to hear a loud pop. Damn it, I have a blowout. The car starts sliding as I lose traction.

Headlights appear seconds before I sideswipe the oncoming car. The screech of metal as my front clips the other vehicle's back end is deafening in the silence of the night. I come to an abrupt stop when the front of my car plows into a snowdrift. It takes me a few moments to catch my breath, and then I'm grabbing the flashlight I was sensible enough to keep on the front seat.

I move out into the freezing snow.

The other vehicle has skidded off the road. The small car's back end is the only part visible. I slip and slide to the car. I'm hoping it's in a small ditch and the car doesn't fall further.

I can't get to the driver's door, so I open the trunk just as a woman bundled in a hat, scarf, and long down jacket tumbles from the front into the back with a loud "Oomph."

"Are you okay?" I shout. "Grab my hand."

The woman rights herself and then tilts her head upward. "Get me out of here, please," she says, her voice bordering on panic. Her trembling hands reach forward.

Grasping them in mine, I help her climb from the car just as a sheriff's car approaches. "I called him," she mutters.

"Good. Do you need anything from inside?" I glance toward my car and wince. "We both need a tow."

"I agree." Her voice wobbles as she snatches her hands from mine and rubs at her forehead.

"Did you bang your head?"

"No. I'll be bruised tomorrow from the belt, but nothing worrying."

"I'm sorry. My tire blew," I admit, glancing back at my car. "I'll cover everything. Don't worry." I look at her small car, which I'm sure has seen better days before the accident.

"You don't need to do that. Tonight wasn't your fault, nor mine."

I don't bother arguing with the stubborn woman as the sheriff joins us. Plenty of women I know would gladly let someone else pay their expenses. I don't even know this woman, and she already has my respect even though I'm a little bit irritated with her.

It doesn't take long to sort everything out, including being breathalyzed. I don't mind because the zero-alcohol level will show up, and the sheriff won't be wondering if I've been drinking. The road now clear, I climb into the back of the sheriff's car with the woman.

"I'm taking you to the clinic for a checkup. Then I'll get you both a ride home." He pauses. "Are you staying in town?" His question is directed toward me.

"Blossom Creek Inn. I have a reservation."

Silence proceeds my answer, and the woman not

once looks at me until we get inside the clinic. We find ourselves perched on the two beds in the small examination area.

"I'm Beatrice Leonard. I own the deli in town." The woman introduces herself as she yanks her wooly hat off, and my eyes follow the trail of dark hair as it falls over her shoulders.

I lift my gaze to her face and pin her with a dark stare. A slight blush coats her cheeks as I say, "Ryker De La Fuente."

"Oh." She smiles. "Are you Levi and Emma's brother?"

"Cousin."

She nods. "You have other family in town?"

I laugh. "An uncle and aunt. I'm not sure if there are others coming."

"Large family, huh?"

"Yes. You?"

"No. Just me." She shrugs. "Hence, why I have, um, had a small car."

"I know it couldn't be helped, but I am sorry. I'm just glad you weren't seriously hurt."

"Thank you for helping me get out of the car." Her voice wobbles. "The thought of being stuck inside it makes me feel sick."

"Your car doesn't have much protection in these

conditions," I comment and catch a spark of annoyance in her eyes. "Sore topic, huh?"

"Friends have told me that, more than once."

"I'm going to arrange transport for you. The only thing I want you to say on the matter is, 'Thank you, Ryker.'" I grin as Beatrice bristles.

"No arguing in my examination room," the doctor says on entering.

"I'm fine, Doc," I say. "She needs looking over. Her car went front first into a ditch. I'm guessing seatbelt bruising."

"I'm not a child," Beatrice snaps. "I can speak for myself."

"Then tell me I'm wrong." I hop off the bed and move closer.

She squirms as I hold her gaze, and admits, "I'm sore from the seatbelt." Narrowing her eyes, she adds, "Not that it's any of your business."

"Now, Beatrice." The doctor pats her knee. "This gentleman is only trying to help."

I can't help the smirk on my lips at the way the doctor chides her. "I take it you've known her a long time?"

"I brought her into this world," the doctor says with delight.

Beatrice clears her throat. "I'd prefer privacy while you check me out."

"I don't mind checking you out with the doc in the room." I tease.

The doc chuckles. "I think her comment was meant for me."

Grinning, I waltz to the door. "As you wish."

An hour later, cold, tired, and frustrated, I crash on the bed in my room at Blossom Creek Inn and curse my life.

However, the last image in my head as I drift off to sleep is of Beatrice's pretty face.

## 2

### RYKER

I'D FORGOTTEN WHAT IT'S LIKE TO LIVE IN A SMALL town where everyone knows your business. Blossom Creek isn't my home, yet news had traveled quickly that I'd paid Beatrice's medical bill and purchased her a small SUV. I did it for no other reason than the fact I'd been responsible for her losing her only means of getting around. I know it hadn't been my fault exactly, but I still felt guilty about it. So, yes, I'd paid for the vehicle. It was no big deal. At least to me it wasn't. Apparently, to Beatrice and the rest of the town, it was.

It has been good spending time with my cousins and aunt and uncle here, yet it doesn't explain why I'm still in town.

*What a lie! Beatrice and that passionate kiss you*

*shared the evening of the opening has everything to do with why you're still in town.*

"I'm not going to think on that," I mutter to myself and clear my throat. It has been weeks since Emelia's successfully opened.

My family has certainly been entertaining; they've had the tongues wagging on the gossip wire.

Emma has already moved out of the inn and into the town sheriff's house. Levi has moved in with Vivien Taylor, the chocolate lady. Her sister, Ingrid, has moved into Levi's apartment with Deputy Nathan. For once, it's amusing to hear the gossip without being at the center of it.

Then there's Levi's business partner, our cousin Ryan McKenzie. He and his fiancée, Gretchen, have just announced a surprise pregnancy. The couple are excited, and Ryan is strutting around town in delight. No doubt in his mind about becoming a father.

I'm happy for them.

Taking a sip of coffee, I watch my cousin Levi stroll into Temptations. He grins at his girl before joining me.

"Have you spoken to Bea recently?"

"No. Should I have?" I frown. "I haven't seen her."

Levi smirks. "You have noticed how pretty she is,

right? I mean, I know there isn't anything wrong with your eyesight."

"I'm not in town to make those sorts of acquaintances."

"How old are you?" Levi shakes his head. "Acquaintances? You either want in her panties, or you don't. So, answer the question."

"There was a question in there?"

Levi sits back in his chair and gives me a skeptical glare. "You are avoiding answering." He points out.

Sighing, I admit, "She's pretty, okay? Happy now. I noticed. I would have to be blind not to. She just isn't my type."

*Lying asshole!*

"Who isn't your type?" Vivien Taylor, owner of Temptations and girlfriend to my pain-in-the-ass cousin, asks.

"Bea," Levi says.

"Ignore him, Ryker." Vivien pats me on the shoulder and adds, "Bea isn't looking for romance."

Levi snorts. "That's what I said and look where that's gotten me."

Vivien clears her throat and puts her hands on her hips. "And where exactly has that gotten you?"

The humor is wiped from Levi's face seconds

before he jumps up and takes Vivien's hand. "Excuse us."

Moments later, Ingrid plops down into Levi's vacated chair and rolls her eyes. "Those two are now having sex back there."

I splutter into my coffee at the casual way Ingrid made that announcement.

"Too much information, Ingrid."

The mirth leaves her face and is replaced with worry. She lets out a sad sigh. "My parents are planning on visiting Blossom Creek with the intention of taking me back with them. I'm not going." She nervously bites her lip, then adds, "I'll be twenty-one soon and have started to build a life here with Nathan... I'm worried."

"Legally they can't force you home. You know that, right?"

"I do. But you haven't met my parents."

I continue, "There is no way Nathan would let you leave, unless it were your choice, and neither would Vivien."

Getting quickly to her feet, Ingrid says, "I'm going to call them and let them know I'm no longer living with Vivien. I'll let them know I've moved in with a man." She smirks. "That will tell them I'm no longer a virgin." She runs out of the store.

After Levi bugging me and then Ingrid talking openly to me, I'm wondering if I have "Agony Aunt" written on my forehead.

Baffled by their behavior, I leave Temptations.

I glance up and down the street, inhaling the cold air. It's good at clearing out the lungs, freezes any germs gathering. At least, according to my dad.

I tug my jacket up around my neck and glance at the doorway into Beatrice's deli. A few people stand at the counter chatting with the woman. Bea looks happy, and then she looks out the window and spots me. Her smile freezes on her face before she offers a tentative wave.

Waving back, I find my feet carrying me toward the deli, and then I'm inside. I groan to myself when the people glance between us both.

"Morning," I mumble as I wait my turn.

Beatrice coughs and starts serving. She blushes as the group in front of me gathers their order and finds a seat. I wink at Beatrice and grin as I lean over the counter. "I guess we're the topic of conversation, huh?"

Rolling her eyes, Bea says, "You have no idea what I've had to put up with because you bought me a car."

My brows draw together in a frown. "I didn't

intend to make you the center of gossip. I bought it so you had a way of getting around. I mean, don't you make deliveries?" I wiggle my brows. "Be glad no one saw *you* kissing me in the snow."

She gasps. "You manhandled me and then kissed the life out of *me!*"

"I wouldn't mind kissing the life out of you again." I smirk.

Bea sighs and says nothing more as she pours two coffees. She moves out from behind the counter and indicates for me to follow her toward a table at the back of the store.

"Is it safe to leave the counter unattended?"

"Tracy is there."

I glance back and notice the young woman.

"I do make deliveries, and I am grateful for the car. More than you could know. It makes me a little bit uncomfortable though, accepting an expensive gift from a man I don't know." She shrugs and adds, "I'll get over it."

"Then I'm glad I did the right thing." I glance at the patrons spread through the small deli, probably trying to listen to our conversation. Beatrice wouldn't appreciate me saying something loud and scandalous to give them something more to talk about, so I keep my mouth shut.

"I thought you only planned on being in town for a few days?" Beatrice tilts her head, her beautiful face open and inviting.

I sit back and slouch in the chair, resting my booted right ankle on my left knee, hoping to ease an ache that appears suddenly and swiftly behind my zipper. So unexpected.

"I plan on going back to Great Falls at some point. I'm just not sure when. I like Blossom Creek."

*I'm still here because of you.*

"Great Falls, Montana?"

"The one and only. Born and raised out there."

"Siblings?"

"What's with all the questions? Anyone listening will think we're on a date." I tease, but unfortunately it has the opposite effect.

"I was curious." Beatrice quickly moves to her feet as though she can't get away fast enough. "See you around," she adds from over her shoulder.

*That went well.*

"Until later, Beatrice," I drawl, my voice thick and throaty.

Her eyes widen and I know my words have done what they were meant to. The tongues would be working overtime now. It serves the woman right for running away.

Maybe I need to think about why it bothers me so much that she did run. I was teasing and had expected a different response.

Leaving the deli, I button my coat and hear, "Ryker?" Louisa Ryland jogs up to me. "I thought it was you. Want to grab a coffee?"

"Just had one, but I will take a raincheck." I grin at the bubbly woman with a head full of dark hair. "However, I will accompany you to the door of the coffee shop." I offer her my arm, knowing that Beatrice is watching from behind me.

Louisa slips her arm through mine and off we go, but not before I glance at Beatrice and give her a wink.

Beatrice's eyes narrow and I know I've gotten to her. I'm starting to think that pretending I don't find Beatrice hot as hell is going to be more trouble than it's worth.

Oh, Beatrice Leonard, you are going to be fun to get to know.

## 3

## BEATRICE

HURRYING THROUGH THE CUSTOMERS, I CONTEMPLATE why Ryker showed up to talk to me. I haven't seen him since the opening of Emelia's, and then later that night…

*Do not think about how his lips had felt plundering your own.*

I know he's still in town, but I haven't caught one sight of him. Until today. The dark-haired man with piercing green eyes had been kind to me after the accident. And I love my new car even though I still feel a twinge of guilt for accepting his gift.

If I hadn't needed a vehicle to carry on with my business, then I would have been more than adamant to refuse. I had agreed, so I suppose I should get used to the idea that someone bought me a car. My first brand-new car. Not a piece of junk that I've only ever been able to afford.

Sighing, I grab the bag of tomatoes that need chopping and start on that—something to keep my hands busy.

"Hello, Beatrice. How are you today?"

I turn and smile. "Morning, Maureen. I'm just fine. What can I get you?" Maureen Roscoe has been the postmistress for as long as I can remember, and her husband, "Old" Mr. Roscoe, owns the hardware store. I'm not sure anyone in town knows his first name.

I ring Maureen's order up at the cash register, and she sighs. "I saw that lovely young man walking Louisa across the road." She raises a brow. "I thought he was your young man, Beatrice."

*Here we go. The nosy coot.*

"He is not and never has been mine, Maureen, regardless of the gossip circulating." I smile and exchange goods for money, then I make myself look busy to get rid of her. She's the biggest gossip in Blossom Creek, along with her best friend, Eileen Ryland, who also happens to be Louisa's mom.

I'm not cut out to be gossiped over. I'm much happier being in the background.

"You need a girls' night." Blu Mathis from the

flower shop suggests. "Wine, pizza, cake, and lots of giggles."

"What I need is to pay more attention to my customers instead of woolgathering."

Blu snorts. "Instead of thinking about the hotness of that man, you mean." She grins. "Have you seen the way he fills out a pair of pants and shirt?" Blu sighs and rests her elbows on the counter. Her chin drops onto her upturned hands. "He's dreamy."

"Yes, I've seen him. I was there at the opening too." I shrug. "He will be leaving town eventually. I wonder how many broken hearts he'll be leaving behind."

"His name has only been connected to yours." Blu wiggles her brows. "So, I wonder…"

"Not mine," I snap. "Shit! I'm sorry. I'm a bit touchy today."

"I wonder why." Blu tilts her head to the side and watches me. "You saw him walk with Louisa, huh?" She smiles softly. "He was a gentleman. I may have been listening to their conversation. I mean, it was right outside my store, and the window was open." She chuckles. "He very politely told Louisa that he wasn't interested in anyone."

"I'm not interested, Blu." I glance through the window and smirk. "Shep's on his way in."

Blu quickly jumps and looks toward the door. "Oh God! Do I look good?"

I roll my eyes. "You always look good."

The bell rings and in walks Shep. There is a very slight pause in his step when he spots Blu, who fluffs her hair yet again.

"Bea, Blu," he mutters.

"Hi, Shep, what can I get for you?"

He flicks his gaze to Blu before holding my eyes. "I was wondering if you could do me a favor."

"What kind of favor?"

Shep grins. "Make up a selection of sandwiches and cakes for the coffee shop tomorrow. I'll charge what you do so you'll get full price."

"Is everything okay?" Blu asks.

"I have something to do later and I'm not sure I'll be back in time to get the food made up before the store opens." Shep fidgets.

Noticing Blu opening her mouth to ask many questions Shep probably doesn't want to answer, I quickly say, "That's no trouble. Do you have it written down? Numbers? Flavors?"

He passes me a slip of paper. "Thanks for this, Bea." He quickly kisses my cheek and dashes out.

I'm left in surprise with my hand going to my cheek and a frown forming on my brows. "Don't ask," I mumble to Blu. "I have no idea what that was about. He's never done it before."

"Don't worry about it. It's okay if you like him too."

"Blu." I snap my attention to her. "I am not interested in Shep. I have never been. Maybe he just acted spontaneously in relief that I'd help."

"If you say so." Blu perks up. "I'll arrange our evening." She twirls around and leaves me in peace.

Well, not precisely in peace, considering Ryker pops straight back into my head. That man has a wicked smile, more so when he smiles with his eyes as well.

Ryker fills my head with images of lots of hot and sweaty sex, which in turn makes me very uncomfortable. And I don't know what to think about that or do about it.

## 4

### RYKER

THREE MORE DAYS OF MAKING SURE I CATCH A glimpse of Beatrice is ridiculous. I'm a grown man, for God's sake. Beatrice is also a beautiful woman. Not just on the outside but inside too. I've noticed how she likes to help others without anything in return.

She's a happy person, and I shouldn't be contemplating what I am. Unfortunately, I have baggage that isn't going to go away overnight, no matter how much I wish it would.

Sighing heavily, I swing my eyes back to Beatrice, who keeps casting glances in my direction. She watched me pull up and knows I'm still inside my truck, although she can't see me as I can her.

Today she's wearing a pretty white dress with

small sunflowers printed on the material. Her luscious abundance of hair is tied back in a tight ponytail. The look of delight in her eyes as she chats with her customers. That look changes to caution when she glances toward my truck.

"I'm an idiot," I mutter to no one in particular as I finally climb from the vehicle.

"Are you going inside or planning on standing there all day?" a female asks.

I give the woman a sideways glance and notice it's the woman from the flower shop next door. Her name escapes me.

"I'm going in."

"I'm Blu, by the way." She grins and stands beside me.

"Ryker," I mutter.

"I know who you are. Everyone does."

"Small town gossip, huh?"

"Of course. Plus, I have inside information."

That gets my attention. "What exactly does that mean?" I eye Beatrice through the large bay window, and she's warily watching myself and her friend converse.

"It means that Bea talks to me."

I snort out a laugh. "You're not going to tell me anything, are you?"

"Nope." Blu chuckles. "Go in there and put her out of her misery, will you?" Turning away, Blu goes back to minding her own business inside her store.

*What the fuck!*

I enter Bea's Deli and it isn't until I look at Beatrice that I realize I'm scowling hard. I'm surprised I haven't cracked the counter separating us. I wince and clear my throat. "As the town is already talking about us, I was wondering if you wanted to come over to Emelia's with me after you've finished work?"

I've shocked her. Good.

With a genuine smile on my face, I watch as Beatrice slowly turns a lovely shade of pink, which gets more profound by the minute. I take pity on her and add, "Do you want me to pick you up, or would you prefer to drive yourself?"

She coughs a few times. "I'll meet you there. Seven thirty?"

"Okay." I smirk and reach for a hand. I gently pull her toward me, aware that her customers are watching every little thing, and I kiss the back of her hand. "I'll see you there, *Beatrice.*" I place another kiss on her hand and stroll out of the store, feeling lighter than I have in a while.

Beatrice Leonard is going to be trouble. I rub a

hand over my chest—a sexy bundle of trouble that leaves me wondering what the hell I'm doing.

---

DURING THE AFTERNOON, I'VE HAD TIME TO THINK about what I'm doing, and I have decided I need to spend time with Beatrice as friends. The woman is a breath of fresh air, and I need that more than she'll ever know. I'm not using her because I'm sure I'm obsessed with the woman. I live for those shy smiles she offers when she sees me.

It's because of my confusion over what the hell I'm doing that I'm still wearing the same clothes I've worn all day. It will send a message to Beatrice that I want to be her friend, even though I've imagined her naked and in my arms. More than a few times too.

Levi looks me up and down when he joins me on the porch of Emelia's. I can tell he isn't pleased with me without him having to say anything. He still has to ask, "Why are you wearing scruffy jeans and a T-shirt for dinner with a beautiful woman?"

Rolling my eyes, I answer, "We're dining as friends. Nothing more. Friends don't get all dressed up to go out to dinner."

Levi snorts. "You're an asshole."

"I haven't done anything wrong." I defend myself, starting to feel guilty. "Look," I continue, "the whole town is talking about us, so I figured if I wanted to spend time with a woman, then it might as well be Beatrice." I shrug. "Not the best plan I've had."

"A stupid plan," Levi mutters. "I think there is something wrong with you."

"Can't you go and annoy someone else?" I grumble and slowly move away from him.

He follows and, after minutes of silence, says, "So, Beatrice is aware of this 'just friends' dinner?"

*No.*

"Of course. Why would you ask?"

"Um, because she just pulled *out* of the parking lot, which makes me wonder if she heard your stupid ass talking."

My eyes widen in surprise, and I curse.

Levi laughs.

## 5

## BEATRICE

THERE WAS ME TAKING A SHOWER, FIXING MY HAIR and makeup, making sure my dress fit sexily to my curves. And there was *him,* who couldn't make an effort to change. I'm not a snob or anything, and if he honestly hadn't had time to change, then I wouldn't be bothered. However, I'd been about to step around the corner when I heard Ryker talking to his cousin.

Ryker had sounded like the only reason he'd asked me out was because the town was talking about us already. What an unflattering asshole.

It goes to show that good looks do not necessarily mean a nice person. Well, at least I'm aware of what Ryker is like before the meal went ahead.

My shoulders slump as I make my way into my small cottage. It's neat and tidy with a two-seater sofa, an armchair in the living room, and a four-person setup to one side of the kitchen. I'd scrimped and saved to buy this place and fit the kitchen how I've always dreamed. My refrigerator and other kitchen accessories are in mint green with white cabinets. It's cozy, and I love it. I can't imagine living anywhere else.

I place my evening purse on the kitchen table and stare around, upset that someone would choose to hurt me in that way. I know he hadn't expected me to overhear him talking, but I had. Nothing will change that.

Five minutes later, I'm still standing in the kitchen like a fool when there is a knock at the front door. I don't want to answer because I know it will be Ryker. He has no clue I was there and probably thinks I've stood him up.

Angry and wanting to give him a piece of my mind, I stomp to the front door and fling it open.

*Ryker.*

I don't say anything and raise a brow.

He looks awkward and becomes angry himself as I refuse to speak. He gives in first. "You heard?"

"I'd have to be deaf to have not heard you."

"I'm bored and figured a nice dinner with you would be...nice." He winces. "I didn't mean for you to hear that."

"Ryker," I say, exasperated, "I'm more than aware I wasn't supposed to have heard you. However, I did. You have a brain in your head and a tongue in your mouth. If you asked me out to dinner as a friend, you should have said as such so I'd know. I'm not a mind reader. What did you expect me to think after you kissed me that night?"

"Can we talk about this inside? It's cold."

"No!" I snap. "Stupid me thought you liked me."

"I do like you." He pulls the collar of his jacket up around his neck.

Changing my mind and inviting him inside is on the tip of my tongue. However, I'm annoyed at being used, so I leave him outside.

"I'm tired and hungry. I'm done. Enjoy the rest of your visit here." With that, I slam the door in his face.

I fling my shoes off, wiggling my toes now, they are no longer scrunched up in a pair of heels that make my legs look fantastic. Too bad for Ryker.

Putting him out of mind, I move through my

home toward the bedroom when I'm interrupted once again by the front door.

I peep through the window to the side of the door, and to my dismay, it's Ryker.

*What now?*

"Yes?" I sigh the moment I open the door.

He winces and looks frozen. "My truck won't start. I swear I didn't plan this."

*Heck!*

"You better come in."

He quickly enters and I shut the cold outside. "The radiator over there is on if you need to warm up."

"Thank you."

"Considering you're from Montana, shouldn't you be used to this weather?"

"I've been living in Europe. Hat and scarves are not easy to purchase there. I must shop tomorrow. I've put up with it since I arrived in town, but I've never been out for as long as I have this evening."

"Yes, well, whose fault is that?" I rein in my anger and disappointment and ask, "Do you want to call someone?"

"I've already called Levi to come and pick me up. We'll get the truck tomorrow, if that's okay?"

"That's fine. At least you haven't blocked me in."

He warms up some and says, "I'm sorry about tonight, Beatrice. The thing is"—he turns to face me—"I do like you. A lot more than I want to. I don't want anyone—you especially—involved in what's going on in my life back in Europe." He gives an embarrassed laugh. "I don't think I've admitted that to anyone."

I tilt my head and hold his gaze. "Your family doesn't know what's going on with you?"

"They don't even know something is going on." He shrugs. "It's awkward and I sometimes struggle to understand how it happened in the first place. I know I'm being vague, but I don't want to talk about the problem. I just wanted you to know that it isn't you." His eyes take me in from my feet to the top of my head, missing nothing in between. "We'd already be in bed otherwise."

I shudder.

"Is that honest enough for you?"

"Oh," I mutter, and escape into the kitchen.

Ryker follows. "I can go on if you'd like. If you'd not hate me as much as you do?"

That surprises me. "I don't hate you, Ryker. Disappointed, but hate is too strong a word."

He nods and releases what appears to be a

relieved sigh. "I would like to take you to lunch tomorrow if you'd allow me."

"Friends?"

His eyes flare before he coughs. "Yes. Friends."

Do I want to have lunch with a man I might end up giving my heart to and then have him up and leave?

"It's okay," he says when I don't reply. "I get it." He turns away, and I feel sorry for him.

"Lunch would be great?"

He stops and glances over his shoulder, a smile slipping onto his face. "Really?"

"I'll sort the food out. I mean, I do own a deli." I smile. "Meet me there at one, if that's okay?"

He receives a text message.

"Levi's outside. I'll be there, Beatrice." He reaches the front door and pauses, then turns back to me. "Thank you for giving me a chance at redeeming myself."

He winks and he's gone. Then he knocks and shouts, "Let me hear you locking up in there."

Smiling to myself, I move forward and slip the locks into place. "I'm locked in for the night."

"Sweet dreams, *Beatrice.*"

Sighing softly, I make it to my bedroom, this time playing over and over the way Ryker says my name. I usually prefer Bea and make that known, yet right from our first meeting, I like hearing my full name on his lips.

Perhaps there is something wrong with me. I don't care and grab my pajamas. I'll slip into comfortable clothing and order pizza.

## 6

### RYKER

I ROYALLY FUCKED UP LAST NIGHT AND I HURT THE feelings of a good woman. Of a woman I am attracted to. If I weren't afraid of my life in Europe and life in the States clashing, there would be no confusion. I'd be with Beatrice. The woman has driven me nuts since that very heated kiss behind Emelia's during the opening. It had been a surprise. One that had left me aching with want.

Having that constantly playing in my mind is why I want to be with Beatrice. Perhaps I should have walked away. After I'd purchased her a car, I should have left without looking back.

I hadn't wanted to. As much as I did think about it, the fact is, I like Beatrice. I like how soft her dark hair is and how it smells of peaches. I like her shy smile and the way her cheeks blush when she's embarrassed. I like how she enjoys her customers. Everyone, no matter what they purchase, is treated the same. She smiles a lot. She helps others. I'd overheard Shep from the coffeehouse praising her for helping him out.

Running a hand through my hair, I sigh and continue watching her cut thick slices of freshly baked bread before layering them with butter. My mouth waters knowing that she will be bringing it over to where I'm sitting.

Her bottom lip is sucked between her teeth as she moves toward me. Her blush deepens when she catches my hooded gaze. She places the plate with the warm bread in front of me and a cup of coffee to the side. "I thought this would keep you going. I won't be too long. I just have to wait for Tracy to get back from lunchtime deliveries."

"I have no issue with sitting here eating this delicious-looking bread while I watch you work." I grin.

"Friends," she mutters, giving me her back.

I frown into the plate and shake off the doubt I feel whenever I'm with her.

*Friends.*

*Friends were my idea.*

*Idiot!*

Picking up a thickly sliced piece of bread now dripping in melted butter, I take a huge bite and close my eyes, moaning at the taste. Yeast bread has a unique smell and taste, and the cream and salt in the butter explode on my senses. It doesn't take me long to finish the three slices.

I lick my lips and wipe my fingers on a napkin as a smiling Beatrice joins me. "You either really enjoyed that, or you were starving."

I laugh and stand, tossing the napkin down. "I'd say yes to the first and maybe to the second."

Tracy comes over and tidies the table up, removing the dirty dishes as I take Beatrice by the hand.

Her hand is small and soft in mine as I twine our fingers together. She doesn't hesitate and lets me lead her to the front of the deli. I grab the basket she indicates and then we're out in the cold.

"I have a confession."

She raises a brow.

I continue, "I didn't think about where we could have this picnic." I wince. "I only thought about being with you."

"Oh!"

She lights up at my words and I smile before

clearing my throat. "We can eat in my truck, but outside of town."

Beatrice laughs. "The whole town will watch us if we stay here."

"That's what I was thinking. So, as you live here, where would you recommend we go and eat?"

"If we drive a mile past the turn for Emelia's, there is a left-hand turn that will take us to the top of the field Emelia's backs to. It's higher up and is beautiful in winter. And summer."

"Your chariot awaits." I tease as I unlock the truck.

———

WE EAT IN SILENCE, ENJOYING THE MELTING SNOW and warm sun shining through the windshield. It's still cold and some mornings freezing, but winter is slowly turning into spring.

"Tell me about your family?" Beatrice asks, smiling.

"You might not like me if I do."

She snorts, which she quickly tries to cover up before laughing. "Please, Ryker."

"Okay." I smile. "My mom, Sarah, is a vet and switched to part-time hours a few years ago. My dad, Aiden, has worked the family ranch in Montana since before I was born. My uncles, aunts, and cousins all spend time there. Helping. Lounging around." Chuckling, I add, "My sister Kennedy is a bookworm but loves being on the ranch. She doesn't miss anything, which is good as she constantly insists Dad and Uncle Diego are getting too old to remember *everything*. She can be dramatic."

"I haven't been anywhere, really." She shrugs. "Boston."

"I like Boston."

She smirks. "When I visit, I always purchase a Boston cream donut. I mean, I know you can get them everywhere, but there is nothing better than having one while in Boston. You have another sister, right? I'm sure Levi has mentioned her."

"Yes." I grin. "Valentina is the baby of the family and has been treated as such, so she's spoiled. It's the truth. I don't help either."

"How do Levi and Ryan fit in?" she asks.

"Levi is my cousin. Our Dads are brothers." I pause. "Um, do you know the story about Dante and Emelia?"

"Ah, the priest and the stepsister. Yes. I think it's an amazing love story."

"Anyway," I continue, "Levi and Emma are their

children. Ryan is a McKenzie. Ryan's dad, Ruben, is cousins with my dad. It's much easier just calling each other cousins, you know. Gets complicated otherwise."

"I can see that. Is it nice having a large family?"

I'm thoughtful and answer, "Yes, it is. What about you?"

"My parents were in their late forties when I surprised them." She sighs and twists around to face me. "I was a good kid. I knew what I wanted, which weren't big dreams. I like my life here in the town of Blossom Creek. The deli is the only one in town, so I have a constant stream of customers. I'm content." She offers a soft smile.

"What are you running from, Ryker?"

I freeze at her question. I don't want to be a dick and say nothing when I'm enjoying being here with her. I don't want to deal with the truth either and ruin our lunch. "I'm not ready to talk about it." At least, I haven't lied.

"Okay." Beatrice smiles, but it looks forced. "I need to get back to the deli."

We clean up and then we're driving back toward town when I say, "It's not you," so quietly I'm not sure she hears me. I plow on, "I don't know what I'm doing or how to handle what's happening. I'm here

42

with you because I like you and I want to spend time with you. You mean something to me, Beatrice."

I hear her swallow, then she mumbles, "Thanks for telling me."

Pulling into the closest parking space to the deli, we sit in silence. It's on the tip of my tongue to ask her to dinner as more than friends. It's there and hovering. Instead, I unclip both our seatbelts, cup her face in my hands, and kiss her.

An explosion goes off behind my eyelids the moment our lips touch. The second our tongues slide together, Beatrice groans and grips my head. My heart thuds heavily, and I'm sure every drop of blood is pulsing in my cock.

"More," she groans, climbing into my lap.

"Fuck!" The curse leaves my mouth as the sexy woman gives me all her weight. "We have to stop," I beg while shoving my hands up her dress.

Her bare thighs are smooth and silky, and then my fingers flex on her panty-clad butt. The panties are lacy and dainty, and I take advantage, rubbing her on my dick, desperate for friction.

In the distance, I hear something that sounds like a knock. My brain has gone south with the rest of me. Beatrice nibbles on my earlobe, and I fear I'm about to come in my jeans.

A louder knock sounds.

"I'm about to fuck you in the truck in the middle of town in broad daylight," I say, pressing Beatrice down on my lap to stop her movements. "Beatrice," I whisper in her ear. "Are you okay?"

There's another knock and I'm sure laughter.

"I can't look at him," she whispers.

Which means I have no choice.

Sliding the window down, I grin at Jared. "Afternoon, Sheriff."

"Some are having a better afternoon than me," he drawls. "I figured I needed to break this up before the whole town caught you."

A chuckle burst out of my mouth. "You mean like they did you and Emma?"

Jared blushes and shakes his head. "I think you better take this elsewhere."

"Go away, Jared. I can't look at you right now."

The man grins and laughs all the way back to his car.

"That was fun," I comment.

"Frustrating is the word I'd use." Beatrice climbs back into the passenger seat and quickly puts herself back together. Her eyes glance at my lap before she snaps, "I think you're a bit frustrated too."

"I'm going to take care of this as soon as I get

back to the inn." Grinning, I wiggle my brows. "You could join me?"

"We've gone from picnic as friends, to me not knowing what you want from me, to nearly having sex in your truck. No wonder I'm confused."

"I'll make it clear. I want you like crazy. The chemistry between us is real. I look at you and see a beautiful woman who I want to spend days, weeks, months making love to. I am the one who is confused about whether or not I'm going to hurt you. I don't want to, but I'm not sure I'll be able to stop it."

Giving me a wary glance, she gets out of the vehicle.

Dropping my head to the steering wheel, I breathe heavily for a few minutes. Back in control, I turn the truck around and go to Emelia's.

## BEATRICE

BLU'S APARTMENT ABOVE THE FLOWER SHOP IS COZY. The moment I'm settled in the oversized, bright yellow bean bag chair, I feel sleepy. My friend ignores me as she greets her other guests for the night of wine and chocolate while we gossip.

I'm usually hopeless at gossiping. However, I have a feeling I might be at the center of it after being caught in a compromising position with Ryker this afternoon. Jared had broken us up and saved us both from more embarrassment. We wouldn't have stopped. I hadn't wanted to. Neither had Ryker. I'd felt how much he wanted me. His thick penis was imprinted on my thigh.

"I hope it's my cousin who has you blushing." Emma teases with a brow raised and a smile on her face. "All I've heard since Ryker arrived in town is talk about you and him." She leans closer. "Plus, Jared may have told me how he found you both." Her brows wiggle.

I snort a laugh. "We didn't get as far as I believe you and Jared did."

She splutters. "He's my fiancé now, so we can't be gossiped about." Emma shoves me over, and with some rearranging, we're both on the yellow bean bag chair.

"Have you started the cookbook yet?" I ask, wanting the subject off of Ryker and me.

Emma rolls her eyes. "I haven't had time. Jared keeps me busy." She whispers, "If you know what I mean."

"Isn't he working?" The moment the question is out of my mouth, I have second thoughts. "Don't answer that."

"I wasn't going to," Emma says with a satisfied smile on her face. "Somedays, I'm still in shock that I fell in love so quickly. Jared is a good man, and my love for him is beyond anything… I don't even know how to describe it. It's like I don't want to be without him for even one second. The feeling is alien, yet it's there and going nowhere." She sighs softly. "You didn't answer my original question." She wiggles her brows again.

"We went for a picnic and talked. It was nice."

Emma gives me a sour look. "Nice? What kind of word is that when you are with my cousin?"

"You won't get anything out of her," Blu says.

Louisa Ryland adds, "Have you seen the new fire chief?"

By now, Ingrid has joined us with an apology from Vivien. Louisa owns the bookstore in town, but her sister, Amber, is also absent.

All eyes stay focused on Louisa, hoping for more information, which she finally gives. "He's tall, like over six feet. A tattoo on his back, dark brown hair and hazel eyes."

"How close did you get?" Blu asks.

Louisa sniggers. "Close enough to ask him his name…while he was washing down the engine…*shirtless!*" She grins. "Luke and Jason caught me drooling over their boss."

"Are you blushing?" Ingrid whispers.

"It's hot in here."

We chuckle at Louisa's comment.

"You haven't told us his name," I say.

"No, I haven't." She pauses and rolls her eyes.

"Zeke Davidson. He's thirty-two. Never been married. Not looking to get married."

"How did you get all that out of him?" Emma asks, her mouth hanging open. "I didn't get that much out of Jared when I first met him."

"It's embarrassing." Her cheeks heat further. "He may have caught me drooling. He was nice about it. Gave me his details. Grinned. Then carried on with the hose."

Blu chokes on her sip of wine. "Hose?" She giggles, making me wonder how many glasses of wine she's already consumed. "How big of a hose?"

Emma nudges me in the side and we both burst out laughing. We're supposed to be grown women. However, all that seems to go out the window when we get together and wine is involved.

Louisa clears her throat, and says, "I've brought you all a book to read, and we *will* discuss it the next time we meet. I mean, this is supposed to be a book club, right?"

"Depends, what book?" Emma eyes Louisa warily.

"It's a romantic suspense, so something for each of us," Louise replies. "Speaking of book club, my mother keeps asking to come along." She cringes. "I thought I would start a book club at the bookstore, then anyone can come. We'll keep this one to ourselves because there is no way I am gossiping with my mother in attendance."

"God no!" I exclaim. "Um…"

Louisa grins. "My thoughts exactly."

"This is exciting," Ingrid says.

"Wait?" Blu startles us. "Ingrid, I do believe Beatrice isn't the only gossip going around town." Blu wiggles her brows and Ingrid lights up like a beacon.

"Don't be shy. Vivien isn't here, so feel free to tell me every piece of juicy gossip about my brother." Emma sits forward.

Ingrid chuckles and after taking a considerable guzzle of wine, she says, "Levi is the best thing to happen to Vivien. I honestly don't have any gossip." She tips her head and a thoughtful look crosses her face. "Oh! They had sex in the back room a few times the other day."

Louisa spits her wine down her shirt. "In the shop?"

Ingrid nods. "I don't think I should have admitted that."

"Don't worry. We'll tell her we got you drunk and made you spill the beans," I say. "And I'm not sure that was the gossip in question." I raise my brows.

Ingrid deeply blushes. "I'm not telling you anything about Nathan."

A knock sounds at the door.

"I don't know who that is," Blu mutters as she goes to open it.

Seconds later, she comes back into the room wearing a huge grin on her face. "It's for you." She looks directly at me.

I wave a hand around for assistance and she hauls me from the low chair.

"You're leaving," she says. "So you'll need to take your purse."

"I'm what?"

"You'll see." At Blu's words, the others scramble up and follow.

My eyes widen at the man standing in the doorway looking sexy as hell. His well-worn jeans fit over his muscular thighs. He's wearing a T-shirt in washed-out gray. When I finally bring my eyes upward, he has the sexiest smirk on his face that I've ever seen.

The man exudes sex.

Emma pushes forward. "Heeeey, Ryfer," she slurs.

His eyes momentarily drift to his cousin. "Emma. I see Jared has let you out to play," he drawls.

"Lonely because he knows I'll be floshed and

getting him ouf of his clothes before he gets me gnome."

I see Ryker's amusement as I'm pushed into him before the door is closed behind me, leaving us alone in the stairwell.

"What is going on?" I ask quietly.

"I have this problem." He takes my hand, and we walk downstairs and out the back door of the flower shop. "You see, since our lunch yesterday, I haven't been able to get you out of my head."

"Oh," I mumble as he buckles me into the passenger seat of his truck.

"It's driving me crazy wondering what you'll taste like. Wondering how soft your skin is. How you'll feel wrapped around me while I move inside of you."

My brain has officially turned to mush.

## 8

## RYKER

I DON'T KNOW WHAT THE HELL HAS COME OVER ME. One minute I'm heading to the shower, desperate for release, and the next, I'm in my truck heading for Beatrice. I wish I could get her out of my head. I can't. She's there and won't disappear. I'm starting to think it's a sign: "Don't let this woman go." So I had gone to find her.

The need is strong, and I don't want to stop *needing* her. She's good and kind, and I want that in my life. I want her.

Coming to a stop at the inn, I turn to look at Beatrice, whose eyes are already on me. "The whole town will know if I take you to my room."

"My cottage," she says with no hesitation.

I force myself to ask, "Do you want me, Beatrice?"

No answer.

"If you don't, I will take you home and leave. I promise."

She glances at my lap and I notice one side of her mouth tilt up in amusement. "That would be painful for you." Her eyes turn soft. "We hardly know each other, but I want you."

"Thank fuck!" With trembling hands, I put the truck into drive and get us to Beatrice's house in no time.

The woman is out of the vehicle and racing up to the front door before I even have my door open. I hesitate to wonder if she's changed her mind and wants to get away from me.

I wait… and wait… and then she appears. "What are you waiting for?"

"Thought you changed your mind," I reply, locking my truck and moving toward her.

"I'm about to have a hot guy drilling into me," she shouts. "Why would I change my mind?"

Too shocked by her words to reply, I let her haul me inside.

The moment the door closes, she's kicking her shoes off and then tossing her dress over her head.

I have to blink a few times. Beatrice in a sexy pink thong and bra is a sight to be savored. So is the way she fills out the lacy bra. My cock has been loaded and ready since I left my room at the inn, and seeing Beatrice in this way has me more than ready to the point of pain.

Eyes not leaving her body and the way she's pinching and rolling her nipples through her bra, I quickly get rid of every last piece of my clothing.

I take my cock in hand, and she gasps. Her eyes widen as she watches me stroke myself and the pleasure that oozes from the tip.

Her thong and bra are tossed to the floor, and then she's on me and in my arms.

I growl as I meet her mouth, our tongues, lips, and teeth clashing together. The feel of her tits against my chest... Her wet pussy rubbing on my dick... It's all too fucking much. My senses overload.

Turning, I push her up against the door, slip a hand between us, and grab my cock and thrust up hard and fast.

"Oh God, Ryker." Beatrice groans against my lips. "Give me more."

Gripping her hips, I press her downward until I'm seated deep and feel her pussy growing thicker, wetter. I force myself not to move because I don't want this over within seconds. She's so close. I'm about to leap out of my fucking skin with how turned on I am.

*What the fuck is it with this woman?*

She wiggles, trying to get me moving. I have no choice as shards of lust slam into me and down my spine, growing in my balls.

Breathing heavily, I slowly withdraw to the tip of my dick before thrusting deep.

"I'm going to come." She pants. A long, drawn-out moan leaves her mouth.

*Yes!*

My hips thrust and shove her into the door. Seconds later, my motions turn deeper and harder, and then I feel the tingle down my spine. I'm not going to last.

I grip her ass tightly and hold her down while I grind into her.

Her nipples are tight buds as they dig into me, and then she climaxes. Intense pulses grip my dick so fucking tightly that I can't last. Semen starts to pour out of me in thick bursts of pleasure. Her pussy is still gripping my shaft as though it's never going to release it.

Even my head and toes tingle from the strength of my release.

Beatrice is collapsed over my shoulder, her heavy breaths vibrating through me.

"You okay?"

"God yes!" She snickers. "I don't think I'll be walking for a week, but I'm good. Can we do that again?"

I laugh and squeeze her tightly. "I hoped you'd say that." Lifting her so that my dick slides out, I wince as my release drips free. Some of it sliding down my cock.

"That's hot." Beatrice meets my gaze. "No regrets?"

"None." I hold out my hand. "Shower and then bed."

She pouts. "I'm not tired."

"Who said anything about sleep." I raise a brow.

"Oh!"

I grin. "I want to bury my face between your legs." I wink. "However, I do not want to get a mouthful of myself. Hence, the shower."

"I wouldn't mind getting a mouthful of you," she comments, moving off into the bathroom.

My head is still trying to accept that *this* Beatrice is the one who is shy and blushes at the barest hint of flirting.

---

BEATRICE HASN'T STOPPED GRINNING SINCE WE WOKE up. She woke me up in a very enthusiastic way, which I better not think about as I have to drive her to work.

This thing with Beatrice is new and exciting. At least, that is how I'm looking at it. I've decided to go for it with the woman I choose.

Beatrice needs to know what happened in Europe. And I'll tell her as soon as I've made a call later this afternoon.

Frowning into my coffee, I feel a headache coming on.

"You look ready to throw that," Beatrice comments, joining me at the kitchen table.

"Sorry. Lost in thought." I force a smile and she sees straight through it.

"We're back to that?"

"No. I will tell you what is going on." I wince. "That's what I was thinking about. I have some calls to make later, and then hopefully, I'll be in a position to tell you everything." I put the mug down.

"Do you promise?"

I take her hands and bring her over to me, onto my lap. Her scent is light and floral and will always make me remember our first night together. I nuzzle into her neck and deeply inhale. "You were hot as fuck last night," I say as a distraction even though I had no intention of bringing it up.

"I like sex." She tries to move from my lap, but I refuse to release her. This conversation isn't over.

"I figured that out."

"You're not going to let me forget how I attacked you last night, are you?"

"Honey," I drawl, "you can attack me like that any damn time. That was the hottest sex I've ever had the pleasure to participate in."

Beatrice laughs deep and dark. "You like my inner vixen. I have no problem doing it, just talking about it. It's a personal experience whether you're scratching an itch or wanting more from the person you are with."

Tightening my grip, I suck her earlobe between my teeth and hiss when her ass grinds on my heavy cock.

"I have to be at work in ten minutes," she whispers, already with her hand between us, unzipping me.

Her cold fingers expose my dick. "Help me."

Realizing what she wants, I haul her dress up and then feel her wet pussy sinking down on me. I grip her waist and grind her down hard. "Get your tits out," I hiss.

Her dress is tossed over her head and then my hands are on her fantastic boobs. I shove her bra down and growl when I get handfuls of flesh, my fingers and thumbs finding her cherry nipples.

"I can't get enough, Ryker," Beatrice says, and then she rides me.

Gripping the table, her hips rock while my cock leaks precum. My appetite for this woman is all-consuming as she grinds and does a hip swirl motion while tightening her pussy. My orgasm is sucked out of my fucking dick without warning.

I squeeze and tug her nipples, and then Beatrice is a shuddering, moaning mess on my lap.

"God, that felt good," she mumbles when she's recovered herself. "I enjoyed breakfast today."

"You better go and dry yourself. It will drive me nuts otherwise knowing you're behind the counter with my cum dry on your thighs."

"You say the dirtiest things to me," she says, shoving her tits back into her bra while looking at my dick.

"You need to disappear before we never leave."

"I hate working."

"No, you don't. You just want me to fuck you all day." I smirk. "I'm not opposed to that idea."

Beatrice groans and, grabbing her dress, disappears into the bedroom.

My lap is wet and sticky. Holding my jeans up, I grab a towel and wet it before cleaning myself up.

Ten minutes later, we're both out of the door.

## 9

### BEATRICE

"I WANT THE DETAILS," BLU SAYS.

My friend was inside the deli the moment I unlocked the door this morning. She leans forward, elbows on the counter and her chin in her upturned hands. There is a large smile on her face, matching the amusement in her eyes.

"I'm waiting," she drawls.

"You look like a panting dog."

"I wouldn't if you'd give me something. Anything. That sexy man came for *you* last night. There is no way you didn't have hot sex with him. No way. It was written all over his face.

"Customers are going to start coming in."

"Then you better tell me quickly." Blu laughs.

"You are impossible, my friend."

She glares. "I'd tell you."

"We had sex. Happy now? It was hot and dirty and so good," I say, getting lost in the memory. "I wish we were still in my bed."

My friend's jaw drops open.

"Please do not drool all over the counter." I grab a pack of wipes and indicate for her to move.

I pride myself on good hygiene as I serve food and drinks, so I wipe down where Blu was loitering.

"Don't you have to open?" I say.

Blu stares. "He likes you."

"I like him too."

"I know that. You wouldn't have slept with him otherwise." She smirks. "Everything would be so good if I can get Shep to notice me as more than a friend."

"If you'd let me drop hints to him, then maybe he would."

"I want him to notice me because of me, not because someone else draws his gaze toward me." Blu looks down, trying to hide her sad smile. "I better go and open up."

Blu leaves and I sigh softly, wondering what I'm doing with Ryker. He has a life in Europe—an exciting, albeit dangerous, life test driving racecars —or at least he did. His family is in Montana. My whole life is here in Blossom Creek. I don't want to move anywhere else. Ryker hasn't promised me anything. Perhaps I need to try and get through to my heart that it's only sex. I'd tried to think that last night, but it hadn't sunk in. It had felt like so much more. I'm confused and don't know what to do.

The tinkle of the bell as the door opens draws my gaze to a heavily pregnant woman. She is stunningly beautiful with dark hair curling down her back and a slight bounce as she walks. Well, waddles. I'd say she was due at any time. She certainly has high-class taste by the look of her clothes, makeup, and neatly trimmed nails. Her purse is Gucci and an original. I only know that because Blu is obsessed with designer brands; I have no choice but to listen to her.

I serve the stranger a sandwich and bottle of water and help her sit at one of the tables in the back. She's polite but nervous by the way she eats and glances around.

Emma arrives and asks, "Who is she?"

I shrug. "No idea." I smile at Emma. "What can I get you?"

She snorts. "So polite when I want the dirt on what you and my cousin got up to last night."

I roll my eyes and chuckle. "You should have been here with Blu."

Her eyes twinkle. "I was having hot sex with my fiancé."

"Jeez, Emma. I do not want to know what you get up to with the sheriff. How do you expect me to look him in the eye when you say stuff like that?"

She laughs. "So, back to my cousin."

I open my mouth to reply but spot the pregnant woman behind Emma.

"Hi," I say. "Is everything okay?"

"It was lovely. Thank you." She twitches and looks around, still nervous it seems. "Um, I'm looking for someone. Well, not just someone. My fiancé. I was wondering if you know him, or where he might be at the moment. I went by the inn, but he's not there."

"What's his name?" Emma asks. "We'll help you if we can."

"Ryker De La Fuente."

I don't hear anything else. She's looking for Ryker. *My* Ryker. No, not my Ryker, *her* Ryker. He's engaged to her, and she's pregnant.

I vaguely notice Emma recover and direct the woman outside. I feel the pregnant woman's eyes on me before Emma steers her out of sight.

Dizziness fills my head and my vision blurs as I grip the counter while shock ripples through me in waves.

"What's wrong?"

"Bea?"

"Bea, hello?" Hands are waved in front of my face.

*Tracy, my assistant.*

"I'm okay," I whisper. "Can you take over?"

"Yeah, sure." I feel her eyes on me as I make my way to the back office, where I slump into the chair. I tip forward and rest my forehead on the desk in front of me. Tears well in my eyes and they slowly roll down my face and drip onto the table.

"Bea," Emma whispers softly, her hand going to my back. "I didn't know. I promise that I didn't know."

"I wouldn't have slept with him if I'd known." I sit up and wipe at my face even though the tears continue to fall. "How could he sleep with me when he's engaged and about to be a dad?"

Emma looks upset as I finally lift my gaze to hers. "I'm confused by this turn of events," she says. "We knew something was going on with him, but he would never say what. Ryker isn't the kind of man to betray the trust of someone. He never has been."

"You saw her for yourself, Emma," I shout. "I admit she wasn't wearing a ring, but you can't mistake her *very* pregnant belly."

"No. You'd have to be blind to have missed that," Emma adds. "I'm going to talk to him. He'll expect me to be nosy."

"It was one night," I murmur. "The best night of my life with a man I liked." I pause. "I'm ridiculous for getting upset."

"What?" Emma says. "Do not say that. I've seen how you and Ryker look at each other. There is more there than a quick fuck. I'll be mad at you if you pretend otherwise. Ugh!" Emma stamps her foot in frustration.

Laughter bursts out of me and I can't stop. Emma gives me a weird look, but I really can't stop laughing. Then I do and it gets ugly. I cry. Not the nice soft cry of a woman, but the ugly cry of one who feels used by a man she was falling in love with.

## 10

## RYKER

"You know," Levi says, "there are extra aprons?"

"You'll lose customers if I help," I grumble, hating cooking.

He eyes me warily like he knows there is something different about me. The smile on my face probably has something to do with it too. I've felt more at ease since being with Beatrice.

Before Levi opens his mouth, I say, "Remember that time I was asked to make us cheese on toast? I set the bread on fire under the grill."

"I remember… Who did you fuck?"

I blink a few times and laugh. "Blunt, Levi?"

"I figured it's best to be blunt. You haven't answered."

"And I'm not going to kiss and tell."

"Who's kissing and telling?" Vivien asks, and when she notices me, her smile widens.

"You know!" Levi accuses, moving toward Vivien.

Vivien laughs and pushes him away. "I know everything. Haven't you figured that out yet?"

"Levi," I state. "Leave your woman alone. Jeez, you're like a busybody."

He snorts. "Spill, or I'll eat your lunch." Levi grins.

I laugh. "You can't talk to her about it. I mean it, Levi. I'll tell you, but you don't say anything to her."

"So, it's someone I know and would talk to, then?" He wiggles his brows.

"Honestly, men!" Vivien snaps. "Ingrid told me he went to get Beatrice from the girls' night."

"Thank God!" He places his hand on his chest and laughs. "I was debating locking you in the freezer if you'd fucked someone else."

"As if. She's the only woman to drive me fucking nuts."

Levi throws his head back and laughs. "Ryker, I hate to be the one to tell you this, but that feeling never goes away once you meet the right woman." He slips an arm around Vivien's shoulders and kisses the top of her head. "If you know what's best, you'll marry that woman before someone else snatches her from under your nose," he adds, and I notice Vivien go still beneath Levi's arm.

I'm surprised and watch as Levi meets my gaze. He tries to hide the panic written all over his face.

Vivien clears her throat and tries to slip free.

"Oh, no you don't," Levi growls.

"I have work," she says, not looking at Levi.

"Fuck this!" Levi cups Vivien's face and rests his forehead to hers. "I wanted to be romantic and unique about it, but fuck it. Will you marry me? I love you. You love me. I want to call you my wife. I want to be your husband. I want to knock you up. I want everything with you, Vivien."

"I don't think I should be here for this," I mutter, amused.

"Don't go anywhere," Levi growls. "I might need a shoulder to cry on."

Vivien is the one who bursts into tears. She throws her arms around his neck and repeats, "Yes," over and over again.

"Can I go now?" I ask.

"Not until you've congratulated us." Levi smirks and pops a glittery ring on Vivien's finger.

I pull Vivien into my arms and take her hand into mine. "That was a desperate proposal," I say to Levi.

"But you make up for it with the bling. Is that platinum and diamond?"

"Yes." Levi removes a laughing Vivien from my arms. "And that was a fantastic proposal."

"It was certainly unique," I add. Needling Levi has always been fun. "Congratulations to you both."

I'm not even sure they hear me when I notice Ryan enter the kitchen. He looks troubled as he looks at me. His eyes briefly glance at Levi and Vivien before he waves me over to him.

"Everything okay?"

"Depends," he mutters. "There's a woman out front. Says she's your fiancée."

Blood rushes around my head, sounding like thunder in my ears. "What?" I choke.

"What the fuck?" Levi is suddenly standing beside me. "He's not engaged." He looks at me. "Do you want me to get rid of her?"

I want to say yes, but I have a terrible feeling about who is out there. Then all I can think about is Beatrice.

My life is so fucking screwed up.

"She isn't my fiancée."

"You know who she is, don't you?" Vivien asks, a gentle look on her face.

"Yeah." In every step I take, heaviness forces my

body through the restaurant to where she waits in the reception area.

Yasmin smiles as though she's missed me and pushes her heavily pregnant self up from the chair. "You're here." She moves toward me and goes to kiss me.

I avoid her touch.

"Why are *you* here?" I ask, and realize we have an audience seconds before Levi stands beside me.

I don't miss the way his eyes widen to saucers when he notices her belly.

"Are you not going to introduce me to your friend? After all, I am your fiancée and the mother of your child."

Levi makes a weird nose beside me until Vivien tugs him away. Then I feel her hand on my face, and Yasmin's face fills with anger.

Vivien doesn't back down, and leaning in closer, she whispers, "We're here if you need us. I mean it, Ryker." She kisses my cheek.

"Who is that woman?"

"Family," I answer before I can stop myself. Then I say, "You haven't answered me. Why are you here?"

"Isn't that obvious?"

"No. It isn't." I take her by the elbow and guide her outside. "Where's your car?"

"I got a cab from the airport. I'm an American as well. If I want to have *our* child on American soil, then I will."

"How much longer?" I ask between gritted teeth.

"Five weeks."

"And they let you fly?"

"Yes." She pauses and looks around. "Can we go somewhere warmer? I also need to lie down."

I don't see any way out of this at the moment, so I guide her to my truck and help her inside. Once she's in the passenger seat, I ask, "Don't you have luggage?"

"I went into town first because I didn't know where you would be. I looked for you at the inn and asked them to hold my luggage. The woman was nice. Then I got a sandwich and a cool drink at the deli. I asked the woman in the deli if she knew where I could find you. She was nice too." Yasmin shrugs. "Another woman was in there and told me where I could find you. She looked pissed. Oh, your cousin Emma says hello."

*Fuck, Beatrice knows!*

"What exactly did you say in the deli?" I ask her carefully, my heart flipping in my chest.

"I told the woman behind the counter I was looking for my fiancé. She looked at my belly and

76

smiled. Then I gave her your name." Yasmin looks thoughtful and adds, "That's when the conversation became forced now that I think about it." She narrows her eyes and glares at me. "Are you fooling around with her?"

"Hell no!" I snap quickly, and luckily my conviction puts a smile back on her face.

The last thing I need is for Yasmin to start on Beatrice. Yasmin is a pain in the ass when she gets an idea into her head. Then I curse again when I remember Emma had been there. Well, no need for Levi to call her now.

I am well and truly fucked.

Of all the places in this town, Yasmin had to go into the deli.

I grind my molars. "We will go to the inn and get you a room for the night, but you are not staying in town. There is no us. Do not tell anyone we are engaged. We are not."

"I thought you'd at least let me stay with you until the baby is born. Don't you want to meet your son?"

I am a total bastard for the quick thought that I would love to meet my son if Beatrice were the mother.

I shake my head.

What I'd like to do is send Yasmin packing.

Beatrice should have heard every little detail from me before Yasmin showed up. This is the last place I expected to see the woman.

I should have expected this though, considering how many calls I've received from her. I kept thinking if I ignored her, she'd latch onto someone else.

I'd wanted to forget everything in Europe and move on with Beatrice. That's what I'd decided the night before. That's why I'd planned on telling Beatrice everything tonight.

Now Beatrice is at the deli thinking the worse shit.

Could my life get more complicated?

## 11

### BEATRICE

Hours after crying my eyes out, I am finally at home with my front and back doors locked up tight. I don't want any visitors tonight, even if they're friendly. I want to be alone to wallow in my misery.

It had been challenging to carry on through the day at work. My skin had been blotchy, and I'd looked as though I had hives. I'd worn my sunglasses for an hour or so after that. Tracy had been a godsend. She'd just known I'd needed her to be the boss today. I must remember to pay her extra at the end of the month.

As for Ryker, well, I haven't seen or heard from him since he dropped me off at work with a toe-curling kiss. I'm not going to think about him.

LEXI BUCHANAN

Tonight, I'm going to be selfish and think about myself.

Steam seeps from beneath the bathroom door, and I carry my large glass of wine inside and turn the taps off. The bubble bath is hot and scented with strawberries.

I place my glass down on the counter and quickly remove my clothes, praying I don't cry again.

Balancing on one foot, I dip a toe into the tub. I grab my wine up and manage to get myself comfortable, and sigh. I love long soaks in the tub, yet I don't ever remember having one with such a heavy heart.

I'm upset and disappointed. I'm angry too. I want to hear from Ryker precisely what is going on, and why he fucked me last night when he has a fiancée and baby on the way.

*Fuck!*

Sending an angry text never turns out well, but I don't care right now. Maybe it's the fact I'm currently on my third glass of wine.

*Me: I need you to come and tell me why you lied to me? Tonight!*

I glare at my phone for five solid minutes until I throw it into my bedroom, my message going unread.

There's a knock on the front door.

I ignore it.

The knock gets louder.

I slosh bubbles and water around in the tub as I sit up and listen.

My phone buzzes, alerting me to a new message.

I drop my head into my hands and cry.

There's a bang on the door now. "Beatrice!"

*Ryker.*

"Shit!"

Water splashes on the floor as I quickly climb out and grab a large fluffy towel.

Another bang hits the door.

"Hang on," I shout, wrapping and securing the towel.

Breathing deeply, I center myself and slowly unlock the door.

The first thing I notice is how tired he looks. I know we hardly slept last night, but he seems... bone-weary.

I swallow and step back. "How did you get here so quickly?"

"I've been sitting outside since you got home from work." He shrugs. "I wanted to talk to you but couldn't decide if you'd be better off not talking to me at all."

Afraid of what he's about to say, I admit, "I need

to know what's going on. I know you didn't promise me forever, but I at least thought you were single!" I end up snapping at him. "And she's pregnant!"

Ryker's eyes quickly trail over me before they go to the door, which he closes behind him after stepping inside.

Backing up, I drop my butt to the sofa and fold my arms across my chest. Then I have second thoughts and drag the throw from beside me and wrap it around my shoulders.

"First," Ryker states, "I'm not engaged to Yasmin or anyone. I've never asked anyone to marry me. Not once, Beatrice. Yasmin came up with that all on her own." He slides his fingers through his hair and tugs.

I stay quiet.

"She's the problem, or rather nightmare, that I'm trying to escape from in Europe. The night I 'supposedly' had sex with Yasmin, I'd been on strong meds. I was on painkillers and antibiotics for a crash I endured during a test drive. My body was bruised and cut." He tugs at his hair.

He continues, "Her recollection of events is that we spent the night fucking." He winces. "My recollection is of drinking in a bar and waking up the following morning with a very naked Yasmin in bed beside me. I have no idea how she got there. I don't remember how I got there. I sure as fuck didn't feel like I'd had a night of sex." He pauses. "And to be more specific, there was no sticky after sex feeling."

I cringe, knowing all too well what that feels like on us both. Instead of crumbling like I want to, I say, "So, she says you fucked her, but you don't think you did? Do I have that right?"

"Yeah." He sits his ass in the armchair across from me. "My friends who know her say she's talking horseshit. They are more acquainted with the woman than I am.

"I believe she lied because the real father wanted nothing to do with her. I've never said much beyond hi to her for a few years. I've never been interested in what she was offering, which is why I'm convinced I'm not the father of the baby she carries. I know I'm not. In my heart, I know I'm not. I honestly don't know what to do about her because, after everything I've said, there is a very tiny part of me that wonders what if I am the father?"

Reaching up, I wipe at my slow tears and stare at Ryker. "Why did you spend the night with me?"

His eyes swim with emotion and he swallows hard. "Because you're the woman I want to be with," he says, his voice hoarse. "Everything between you and me was real, Beatrice. Every second. I didn't want the words of another woman coming between us. I didn't want to lose a chance to be happy with you."

"You are saying all the right things, but I can't right now. How do you think I feel knowing you *might* have a baby arriving soon? That the child's mother is staying with you at the inn?"

His eyes widen. "How did you know she was staying with me?" He laughs. "The town grapevine, huh? There are no rooms, and I couldn't let a pregnant woman sleep in her car."

I blink rapidly and murmur a soft, "Oh."

Ryker stares.

"I didn't mean as in the same room as you, but thanks for clarifying that."

His shoulders sag.

Standing on shaky legs, I move toward the door and open it. "Thank you for telling me what happened."

"Is that it?" he asks, his voice tight.

Surprised, I ask, "What did you expect me to say? Did you expect to carry on where we left off this morning?" I curse under my breath. "I have never been known as the 'other woman' before and I refuse to be now. So, please leave."

"Beatrice, please don't do this." Ryker reaches for my face, but I move away.

"I want you to leave."

"Just like that?"

"You made me fall for you and then tore my heart in two. So yes, just like that. Leave!" I can't help myself and give him a push out the door.

He turns to say something else, but I slam the door in his face and quickly lock it back up.

My heart wants me to unlock the door and drag him inside. My head knows I've done the right thing. I can't be with someone who has a woman and a baby with them, regardless of what he said.

Like I told Ryker, I'm not ever going to be the other woman. No way.

## 12

## RYKER

IT'S EATING AWAY AT ME THAT SHE WON'T TALK TO ME. I'm more than aware I was in the wrong. But I have this need for her to know how much the brief time we spent together means to me.

Her cottage is bathed in moonlight with only a small glow from her front room window. I've sat outside her cottage numerous times this past week undecided as to whether to stay away or go after the woman.

Beatrice is the one I want to be with, and I don't care if that makes me an asshole. It's what my body and soul want.

*I'm going in!*

With more conviction than I feel, I put one foot in front of the other until I'm standing at her front door. My heart pounds and blood rushes around my head as I raise my hand and knock.

*That was too soft.*

I knock again, louder.

There is a shuffling noise inside the house, telling me she's there and looking through the peephole. I hold what I think is her gaze and sigh when the locks start to slide.

"You're beautiful," I whisper the moment my eyes land on her. She's wearing a robe and her hair is twisted up with a large black clip holding it in place. Whisps of hair fall around her face and I continue staring.

The words I've wanted to say get lost as my eyes take in every inch of her, knowing she's likely naked beneath the robe.

"You shouldn't be here," she says softly.

My gaze lifts to hers and that's when I notice the tears swimming in her eyes.

My face falls and without thought, I step inside her home and wrap my arms around her. I kick the door shut with my foot.

She stills at first and then I feel her arms wrap around my waist. Her hands splay on my back and grip tightly as she nuzzles into my neck.

"I'm so fucking sorry, Beatrice." I cup her face

and force her to look at me. "You must know that I want to be with you. I choose you. I did the night I took you away from your friends and made love to you." I kiss her forehead and let my lips linger. "I've never touched Yasmin," I say.

She tries to pull away, but I keep her in my arms. "I swear to you, I haven't."

"You remember?"

I want to tell her yes, but… "I don't remember anything and I'm not sure I will at this point." I take her hand and place it over my heart. "I know in here that I didn't fuck her."

Beatrice swallows, and says, "What happened or didn't happen isn't what I'm so upset about, Ryker. Everyone has a past. I didn't know you existed before you came to Blossom Creek. It's the fact you didn't tell me what was happening in your life before we slept together. You let me find out in a way that hurt me a lot more. Do you understand that?"

"Yes! It's hurting me too."

Reaching up, she presses a hand to my face and my eyes find hers. I should really think things through first, but yet again, I don't.

My lips find Beatrice's, and when she gasps, I take further advantage and consume the woman I love. Mere seconds later, I feel her fingers sliding through my hair as she holds me close. Her body slamming into mine.

I make quick work of her belt and have the robe open with my hands on her naked ass. I massage and squeeze the flesh as my mouth sucks and nips down her neck until I can tug on a hard nipple. Beatrice groans and throws her head back, giving me access to her body.

"Ryker," she hisses, "what are we doing?"

I tug and lap at the other nipple. "I'm loving you."

"Don't stop, then." Her hand yanks open my jeans, and I nearly become an embarrassment as her fingers wrap around me. She jerks, hard and fast, and I can't wait a moment longer to get inside her. I'm not coming on her hand.

Hauling her up into my arms, I look around and decide the rug will have to do. With a bit of a struggle considering my jeans are around my thighs, I get us to the rug.

I tremble as I tell her, "Put me inside you. Now. *Fuck!*" The second I feel the entrance of her wet pussy, I thrust hard.

Her eyes widen as her whole body clenches, her pussy rippling as her climax rushes through her. I lower my head to her neck and thrust hard again, and hold still, grunting through my own release.

*That was fast!*

"We can't do that again," Beatrice whispers. "I can't." She starts crying and I don't know what the fuck to do. "I don't regret what we've just done," she continues, "but we can't."

I slip from her body, and kneeling between her legs, I quickly tuck myself away and pull her robe over her flushed skin. She watches every move I make.

Swallowing hard, I pick her up from the floor and sit in the armchair. I cradle her in my arms while she cries, and I whisper, "The one and only thing I regret with you is not being completely upfront to begin with. But I need you to really listen to me, okay?"

She keeps her head buried in my chest, and I say, "Beatrice, please look at me."

Letting out a shuddering breath, her watery eyes meet mine.

"I want you. I'm going to do everything I can to make sure you believe that. No matter what the truth is about the baby, I am still going to be coming after you. I will do the right thing by the child, but I am not now, or ever, going to be with Yasmin. I need you to believe that, even if you don't believe anything else."

After placing a lingering kiss on her cheek, I say, "I'm going to go now before I talk you into letting me stay with you. I know you'll be mad at yourself if that happens, and probably me." Before I close the front door, I say over my shoulder, "Wait for me."

It kills me to walk away from her tonight, but it's what I have to do. I know that. She knows that. I want to come back to Beatrice when I know the truth about the baby.

I meant every word I said to her tonight.

## 13

## BEATRICE

AFTER BEING AWAKE HALF THE NIGHT, I'M SURPRISED to discover I'm feeling happier today. My customers have noticed too, so has Blu, who had watched me like a hawk all through lunch. I haven't told her anything and I'm not going to.

What happened last night was very personal between Ryker and me. You can't get more personal than sex, but that isn't what I mean. The words he said had come from his heart. I'd have had to be blind to not realize that. I'd thought about those words all day and I wanted to talk to him. I hadn't said much last night because I knew I'd be a blubbering mess if I had. I'd ended up that way anyway.

The glass of wine Louisa had poured me as soon as I entered Love Between the Pages is going down rather well, which makes me glad I'm not driving tonight. Emma and her fiancé, Jared, are giving me a lift home along with Vivien. Luckily for Blu, she lives five minutes away.

There has been a lot of interest in Louisa's book club at her bookstore, which pleases me immensely. She's talked about it on and off for the two years she's owned the store. Our girls' nights were originally supposed to be a private book club to discuss books. However, we had a habit of discussing what was going on and with whom in the town instead.

Next to arrive is Louisa's sister, Amber, with their mother, Eileen. Maureen Roscoe, Eileen's best friend, is close behind. I think they'd grown up together.

The Matthew sisters follow—Wynter, who runs the small library, and Summer, the art gallery. Blu rushes in nearly bumping into the sisters and makes a beeline for me.

"What's the hurry?" I ask.

"Shep looked at me." She gushes.

I know what she's talking about, but I tease. "He always looks at you."

"*Bull!* He looked. We were talking as we both were outside locking up. He came over and he stared at me. Like, stared as though he was seeing *me*. Not Blu Mathis. But a sexy woman."

I grin. "Sexy, huh?"

"Of course, I am." Blu huffs.

Amused, I hug Blu. "I'm happy for you."

"Now, all I need is for him to ask me out," Blu says, disappearing to snag a glass of wine.

Louisa clears her throat. "Everyone, find a seat so we can get started." Beaming, Louisa watches the small crowd, and adds, "Thank you all for supporting me and coming to my store for its first book club."

"Do we have a name?" Maureen asks.

Amber asks, "A name for what?"

"The book club, of course," Maureen answers.

"Um, what's wrong with book club?" Summer asks.

"We need something exciting," Blu says.

The bell jingles and rushing inside looking awfully flushed is Judith Carter, owner of Blossom Creek Inn and mother of Blu's obsession, Shep, otherwise known as Shepard.

"No need to have rushed, Judith," Louisa says. "Help yourself to a glass of wine. There a seat available beside Blu."

"I wasn't rushing." Judith takes a glass of wine

and sits in the seat mentioned.

Eileen comments, "You're out of breath."

"You would be too if you'd just discovered the new fire chief."

Blu chokes on her wine while my eyes meet Louisa's. A few others titter.

Wynter asks, "What's so special about him?"

Judith gives her an incredulous glare. "You obviously haven't seen him yet."

Blu swipes another glass of wine and knocking it back, takes another. I smirk in amusement as she whispers, "I need to be drunk to listen to my future mother-in-law talking about hot firefighters."

Now it's my turn to splutter my drink over myself. I give her a dark look with no meaning behind it. She's too funny.

"He's a fine-looking young man," Maureen says.

"Tall, dark, and handsome. He has that stubble thing going on, and his smile..." Dorothy adds dreamily. "His smile melted my knees, and they haven't been melted in a very long time."

Blu snorts. "Blossom Creek Gossips!"

All heads swivel in Blu's direction, who loudly burps. I smother a giggle behind my hand and Louisa rolls her eyes. "Does anyone know if Teagan is joining us?"

"I asked her," Amber says. "She told me she'd be working, but she'd try and come to the next one."

Teagan and her brother, Travis, own the Tremayne Tavern, a bar that serves beverages, appetizers, and good music.

"Okay, tonight I want us to enjoy being together as a group while filling in the forms I will pass around. I'm trying to find out what genre everyone likes to read. If you have a book to recommend, or an upcoming book you're interested in, please note that. We need to choose one tonight so I can make sure I order enough copies of it. We also need to read it before the next club meeting."

"That sounds like a good idea," I mumble.

"I still think Blossom Creek Gossips sounds good." Blu hiccups. "We're gossiping about books."

"And hot firefighters." Summer snickers.

"See"—Blu points—"Blossom Creek Gossips."

I whisper out of the corner of my mouth, "Have you had too much wine?"

Blu hiccups once more.

"How about Wine and Book Club?" I suggest.

"Hmm." Louisa screws her eyes together, then says, "Literature and Wine Club."

"Perfect!" I clap my hands and the others follow.

"I still think Blossom Creek Gossips is the best

name," Blu mutters beside me.

"It is, but we can't call ourselves that. What will the town think? We'd be the ones being gossiped about."

Dorothy pipes up. "Before we get all proper, does anyone know anything about the fire chief? I didn't even catch his name because his eyes held me prisoner."

Blu gives a drunken giggle. "Louisa has all the details."

Eileen gasps. "Louisa? Do you know this young man and you haven't told your mother?"

Louisa blushes and sighs. "His name is Zeke Davidson and he's thirty-two. He's also not interested in single females falling at his feet."

I notice her sister, Amber, has a brilliant grin on her face, "Of course, you know that."

Louisa clears her throat. "More wine anyone?"

Eventually all the wine is guzzled, and we still haven't selected a book for our first official meeting. It seems everyone was more interested in discussing Zeke Davidson.

I can honestly say that I had fun and I hadn't thought about Ryker once the meeting had started.

The town now has a Between the Sheets Book Club based on unanimous drunken voting.

## 14

### RYKER

I've purposely avoided Beatrice for three weeks. It hasn't been easy, and my temper has been on a slow simmer.

Yasmin has decided Blossom Creek is a charming place and wants to give birth here. I've tried to persuade her to go to her family in New York. Yet, she's still here. I can't blame her really as I prefer Blossom Creek too.

I think Yasmin has finally accepted I will never be in her life. She knows if the baby turns out to be mine that I'll support them. I'm already doing that I suppose. Of course, I'll be a dad. That won't change how much I've fallen in love with Beatrice.

When Yasmin's guard is down, I see the fear on her face that I assume has to do with giving birth. It's one of the reasons why I haven't found somewhere else to stay. Even though she's fucked everything up by coming here, I do feel sorry for her in that respect.

I've tried to get her to tell me the truth, even promising I will still be there for her. She will have none of it.

The night before my two worlds collided, I hadn't been thinking about anything other than being with the woman who had captured my heart so quickly and thoroughly. Of course, Beatrice didn't know this, unless she'd really listened to what I said the last time we spoke—the last time I'd had my arms around her.

It would soon be over with Yasmin. She is due anytime, and after some persuading on my part, I'd gotten her sister's phone number. So, Paula is expecting her sister and new nephew to arrive a few days after the birth. It was all sorted much to Yasmin's frustration.

Turning the engine off at the converted barn where Levi lives, I sit for a moment, hoping he'll talk to me.

Levi had been pissed at me and wanted to know what the fuck I was doing. I haven't told him as he's ignored me.

With heaviness in my heart, I climb from my truck and hear the sound of wood being chopped.

Curious, I follow the sound and find Levi behind the building, indeed chopping wood of all things. He eyes me and carries on.

"You can't ignore me forever."

"Try me," he hisses. "I'm still pissed at you."

"I'm still pissed at me, so join the club."

Levi slams the ax into the trunk base and turns to me, his face filled with anger. "You broke the heart of a good woman. You lied to her!"

"Technically, I didn't lie."

Levi's fist slams into my face so hard I lose my footing and end up flat on my back.

*Fuck!*

I close my eyes and breathe through my nose. My jaw pulses like a bitch.

"You going to get up and hit me back?"

"No," I grumble. "I deserved that."

Levi pauses and then bursts out laughing. "Get up." He offers a hand and pulls me up.

I eye him warily, and say, "I was an asshole. You offered me an ear, and I told you to leave me alone." I wince. "In my defense, I'd just spoken with Beatrice. I was hurt."

Tightening his jaw, Levi narrows his gaze. "What is she still doing in town?"

"Wants to have her baby here."

"I noticed you said 'her' and not 'our.'"

I rub my jaw. "I'm doing what I think is the right thing." I blink tears back as I gaze over the rolling hills with snow on the peaks. "What I want is Beatrice. That's it." I shrug. "If I'd gone home, I wouldn't be so screwed up. Yes, Yasmin probably would have followed me to Montana, but Mom would have gotten the truth out of her by now."

"Vivien thinks the truth will come out in the end. Me, I think you should get the truth while she's distracted with labor."

"That had crossed my mind. However, I'm not that cruel."

He gives me a skeptical look. "She's ruining your life and doesn't care. How is that not being cruel?"

"I'm getting a headache… Will you feed me?"

Rolling his eyes, Levi moves inside, and I follow.

"You have a good right hook." I wince and find a bag of frozen peas in my hand.

"I'm not apologizing. You deserved it."

I grunt in response, and ask, "How is she, Levi?"

He grabs tubs from the fridge and places them on the counter between us before answering. "She's pale and not sleeping. I don't think it helps that Yasmin goes into the deli once a day."

"She what?" I shout. "Sorry. I didn't know that."

"Emma thinks she knows about Bea, so she's being a bitch about it."

"I haven't told Yasmin a damn thing about my life here."

Levi adds, "It's the way she speaks and watches Bea when she's there that made Emma comment about it." He passes me a dish with cold pasta and a red sauce.

I turn and shove it in the microwave. "I miss her," I admit quietly as I watch the digital timer count down. "I hardly spent a lot of time with Beatrice, but I miss her, Levi."

A large hand lands on my shoulder and he squeezes. "I admire you for being good to Yasmin. As soon as the baby is born, you need to get a paternity test done. You need to know the truth, whether you like the results or not."

"That's already planned."

"What will you do then?" he asks.

"I've told Yasmin I will help support her and the baby if it's mine. I'll be in his life. She knows I won't ever be with her. I've arranged for her to go to her sister's a few days after the birth."

"Good to know." Levi sighs and gives me an odd look.

"What?"

"When you asked about Bea, I wasn't entirely truthful."

My brows draw together.

"She's lost weight. Vivien said Bea puts on a brave face, but that she's unhappy."

"And it's all my fault."

I check my phone and my heart drops.

"Fuck. She's in labor." I look at Levi.

My feet are frozen to the floor because I do not want to do this, but yet, I know I have to.

Levi shakes me. "I'll come with you."

Instead of climbing into my truck, we climb into Levi's. He heads toward town. "Where am I going?"

"The inn."

## 15

### BEATRICE

STANDING OUTSIDE THE DELI, I LIFT MY FACE TOWARD the sun and close my eyes. The sunlight is nice and warm on my skin, and it reminds me that summer is around the corner and that I can no longer go on the way I am.

My heart is fragile, but I need to start feeling again. I haven't been myself and that needs to change. I'm sick of feeling heartsore.

My lips spread into a smile and I release a slow sigh, feeling better in myself. With the smile still on my face, I open my eyes and find a man standing staring at me. Not just any man. Zeke Davidson. The fire chief. We've never met, but I know all about him from Louisa.

He grins at me and says, "You have a beautiful smile."

"Thank you." I clear my throat and offer my hand. "I'm Beatrice Leonard."

He wraps his large hand around mine and introduces himself. It's on the tip of my tongue to tell him I know who he is, but I refrain.

"What do you think of our little town?" I ask, trying to be polite as he continues to hold my hand.

He slowly realizes we're still attached and let's go with an embarrassed smile. "It's quaint. It reminds me of where my grandma lived when I was growing up. I'm comfortable here." He frowns. "If that makes sense."

Nodding, I say, "It does. I can't imagine living anywhere else. I mean, I love my trips into Boston, but I'm always glad to be home."

"I felt like I was coming home when I moved here. I can't explain it." The man looks surprised at admitting that bit of information.

"Then you made the right decision…" My words trail off as two women walk past, their eyes on the tall firefighter. I chuckle. "The female population sure likes your arrival." I tease.

He blushes but looks annoyed.

"I'm sorry. I shouldn't have said that."

"Don't worry about it." He runs his fingers through his close-cropped hair and says, "It's an annoyance."

"They'll get over it. You're something new to look at." I shrug. "It's just the way of things in small towns."

"So, do you sell anything gluten free?"

Taken by surprise but happy he's asked, I direct his gaze to the storefront. "The cakes and sandwiches in the glass case are all gluten free. I also have a separate workstation in the kitchen that is only for gluten-free items."

"That's good to know." His face lights up. "I'm sick of my own cooking."

"Do you eat gluten free by choice?"

"I have celiac disease. I miss pizza."

Brakes screeching turns our gaze in the direction of the inn. Ryker jumps out of Levi's truck and runs inside.

"I wonder what's going on over there?" Zeke mutters.

We both stand watching. We're not the only ones either; others have stopped on the sidewalk to watch.

Not five minutes later, Ryker comes out of the

inn carrying Yasmin. He places her in the backseat and climbs in after her. Levi takes off.

"She's in labor," Zeke says.

I'm frozen on the sidewalk while my heart crumbles at my feet. Seeing Ryker taking care of Yasmin makes me realize I'll never have that with him. He's chosen the mother of his child, and I don't blame him. It hurts like hell and I feel seconds away from another meltdown. Having his relationship with Yasmin slapped in my face wasn't something I needed. Not now.

*He said he chose you. To wait for him.*

Zeke puts a hand on my arm. "Are you all right? You've gone white."

"I don't—" Pain as I've never felt before cuts off my words as I gasp and fall toward Zeke.

My breath is trapped in my lungs as Zeke lowers me to the ground. I grip his wrist so hard that my fingers will probably be imprinted on his skin. The fire in my side hurts. It hurts so much.

"Bea, honey. Look at me," Blu says.

I see her, but I can't talk.

There's wetness between my legs, which only briefly crosses my mind as another stab of pain ripples through me.

"My car's there. It will be quicker than an ambulance." Blu disappears while Zeke continues cradling me in his arms.

Blu returns holding a blanket. She wraps it over me and then Zeke lifts me into his arms. He places me in the back seat, then climbs into the car with Blu, and we head toward the hospital.

"It hurts bad," I moan, tears streaming down my face. "What's wrong with me? I felt fine this morning." I can't go on as I curl into myself, scared and lonely.

The car comes to a stop, and again Zeke lifts me into his arms. He holds me tightly against his chest as he talks to someone. Then I'm lying on a gurney. I hear Blu say, "Pain and bleeding."

*I'm bleeding?*

Large tears fill my eyes and fall as I'm wheeled away. Then I'm asleep and everything turns dark.

---

THE LIGHTS ARE DIM AS I SLOWLY WAKE UP AND FIND the pain has gone. I feel slightly lightheaded as I look around the room. I'm alone—the story of my life. I wasn't, though. I do remember that. Blu and the friendly fire chief had brought me to the hospital.

*Why?*

*Why did I need to come to the hospital?*

My hand slowly slips across my belly as I remember the pain. The wetness between my legs. It had been blood.

A nurse comes into the room and notices I'm awake. Without a word, she moves closer and offers me a sip of water through a straw. It feels good in my dry mouth and going down my parched throat.

"What happened?" I ask, afraid that I know.

"I'm Marie, your nurse. Do you remember why you were brought here?" she asks softly.

"I was in pain," I answer.

She takes my hand and says, "I'm sorry, honey, but I'm afraid you had a miscarriage."

I'm like a faucet with tears constantly streaming down my face. I can't help it. I'd been pregnant with Ryker's baby and hadn't known it.

"I didn't know," I whisper. "How could I not know I was pregnant?"

"You weren't far along and shouldn't have had so much pain. However, there was an issue with a fallopian tube."

"Can you sit me up a little bit, please?"

The nurse kindly moves the top part of the bed upward, and I feel better. "What exactly happened?"

"The doctor should be the one explaining this,

and he planned to. However, there is an emergency in another part of the hospital that he had to attend to. You had twins growing in your right fallopian tube. Luckily, the tube didn't rupture, but it was a close call." She pats my hand and passes me a tissue. "I'm so sorry for your loss, honey."

"Thank you for telling me." I keep everything inside of me until I can't anymore and start crying.

Through my tears, I see someone come into the room. I think it's Blu, but it turns out to be Emma.

She doesn't say anything as she kicks her shoes off and climbs onto the bed with me. She takes me into her arms and lets me cry all over her. She cries too.

## 16

### RYKER

Yasmin has taken every pain reliever offered, and I feel like strangling the woman or the nurse. I can't decide which. The nurse is constantly calling me Yasmin's partner or asking stupid questions about "how Dad's doing." I want to scream. I don't want to be here.

I want to be with Beatrice, asking her why the hell she was smiling and talking to Zeke Davidson. I'd noticed. Jealousy had ripped through me and I found it was eating at me. I need to know if he's moving in on the woman I love. Realistically, I know that I have no right to be pissed. Yet, I can't help it. She has a right to be happy. I just want her to be happy with me. Regardless of what happens over the next few days, I'm still going after Beatrice. Zeke is a friend and a good guy; I know he isn't looking for anyone.

I'm a bastard for thinking so little of Yasmin and refusing to acknowledge that I'm her baby's father. If I had any recollection of fucking the woman, then perhaps I wouldn't be so suspicious.

"Why won't you talk to me?" Yasmin suddenly asks, the beeping from the baby monitoring equipment becoming regular.

"I'm thinking."

"You hate me?"

I sigh. "If you fucked my life up with lies, then I won't be forgiving, Yasmin. We'll know in a few days."

She looks away toward the door and her eyes widen in shock. I frown and turn toward the door.

I have to blink a few times to know I'm not imagining Derek Patterson standing in the doorway. I'm shocked to see him. And then, as I glance at Yasmin, it all clicks into place.

*Fuck!*

I slowly get to my feet, then I take hold of Yasmin's face and draw her gaze to me. "Is he the father?"

Tears fill her eyes, and although I have my answer, I wait, needing to hear the words.

"Yes," she says. "I'm sorry, Ryker. You never fucked me."

A growl comes from the doorway, and I turn to face him.

"Why the fuck did you disappear?" I ask.

I'm so fucking stupid for not putting it together before now.

"I didn't want a wife and a baby," he says. "Then, after months of running, I thought better of it and went back for her. She'd already left to come here."

"You want us?"

"Yes," Derek states without hesitation.

I turn to Yasmin and laugh. "You do realize that there is a very high chance your baby will have the same skin tone as his *father*? How did you expect to get away with that?"

"I didn't. I'm scared to death of bringing a baby into the world and I didn't want to do it alone. I knew you'd find out either at the birth or afterward."

Anger is a fierce emotion, and before I can say what I want to, I walk out. I pause in the doorway and say to Derek, "I'll leave all the baby's shit she's bought at the inn's reception desk. Collect it from there."

I don't look at Yasmin. I'm too pissed at the woman as I stride through the quiet hospital. Full of anger, I don't see Jared until I'm seconds from plowing into him as he steps into my path.

Closing my eyes, I inhale deeply and slowly exhale. I open my eyes and look at him. I frown. "Emma?"

"Emma is fine, although I am waiting for her."

"Why is she at the hospital?"

He hesitates, then says, "She's with a friend." He holds my gaze, but I'm not sure what he's trying to tell me.

"I'll be off then as long as Emma is okay."

He nods and watches me leave the hospital. It isn't far to town from here on foot, so I set off walking.

My head and heart feel so much lighter knowing I was right. After months of being hounded by the woman, all it took was for Derek to walk into the room and the truth came out. I could have punched him for putting me through that.

I saw not one inch of guilt in her eyes when she admitted the truth. Not one. She'd fucked with my life and she had zero guilt over it.

Angry at being used in that way, I desperately wanted to find Beatrice and tell her about the new developments. Tell her how much it hurt not being able to be with her.

My mother would say I needed to have faith. I sure needed a lot of it if I was going to get Beatrice back.

Before I know where I'm going, I find myself standing on the sidewalk outside Beatrice's cottage. No lights are on and her car isn't here. I'm not sure how long I stare at the quaint cottage, but eventually my feet carry me into town and to the tavern.

Inside is always neat and clean, the brass and wood going well together. I've unwound in here a lot recently—an escape from what waited for me at the inn.

Travis gives me a nod and pours out a smooth malt whiskey instead of my usual longneck beer. "Figured you'd need something stronger."

"That I do. Thanks." I take the drink and sit in a booth in a dark corner. Being left alone to drown my sorrows sounds good.

Tomorrow I'm going to plot and plan a way to woo the woman I'm in love with. I love the woman. Why else would it hurt that I'm not with her?

"Why are you here?"

I glance up, not recognizing the voice.

*Zeke.*

"It's a public tavern."

He rolls his eyes and sits opposite. I've hung out

with the man here more than a handful of times. Played pool in the back too. We've never talked about Yasmin and my fucked-up life.

"False alarm?"

I look into my whisky, wondering what he's talking about. It takes a few seconds for it all to fall into place. "The labor?" I lift my eyes.

He nods.

"No, she might have had it by now."

He rubs his jaw, not able to figure me out, so I add, "The father showed up. Yasmin admitted to lying to me. I knew. Deep down, I knew I hadn't fucked the woman. Don't ask. She fucked everything up."

The rest of the whisky goes down in a fiery swallow as I bang the glass down on the table. "I saw you with Beatrice," I comment, my jealousy seeping out.

Zeke raises a brow. "Now I understand." He refuses to meet my gaze and his face darkens. "I guess I should listen to the town gossip more. Then I wouldn't have missed this."

"What did you miss?"

"That you're the reason Beatrice doesn't smile anymore." He's quiet for a moment. "She'd smile and wave over to us at the station if we were around.

She doesn't even look over anymore. Now I know why."

"You know nothing," I mutter.

Standing, Zeke says, "I can see you want to drink yourself into oblivion, so I'll leave you alone." He hesitates as though he wants to say something more yet chooses not to.

A night with Jack Daniels sounds good.

---

FEELING LIKE SHIT, I HAUL MY STUPID CARCASS FROM the bed and fall into the shower fully clothed. Last night wasn't one of my finest moments. Getting liquored up had sounded good. Now, not so much. It takes maybe ten minutes of holding myself up in the shower for some of the fog to clear. Unfortunately, when it does, I'm not happy with myself.

I push through my morning routine and have to wear dark shades as I make my way over to Shep's coffeehouse for breakfast. Well, for a strong coffee.

The deli hasn't opened yet, which is a surprise but also a relief. There is no way I want Beatrice to see me like this.

It isn't long before the caffeine reaches my veins, and I eventually eat a bagel and have another cup of coffee. More human than I'd felt earlier, I go to the counter and pay Shep.

He hardly talks to me, which is expected considering he's a friend of Beatrice.

On the sidewalk, I inhale the fresh air and feel so much better. I feel alive. I glance at my phone and see a message from Yasmin. More of an apology. She gave birth to a healthy baby boy, who looks just like his dark-skinned father. I am happy the baby was born healthy. But I have no wish to see her again.

The jangle of keys draws my attention to the deli and Tracy opening up. She spots me and gives me a dark look. "You are not welcome here anymore," she says before slamming the door in my face.

*Okay, then!*

Spotting Blu hanging over a window display watching me, I head toward her and just manage to stick my foot into the door before she slams it shut. I curse as pain ricochets through my foot and leg. "That hurt."

"It was supposed to," Blu hisses.

I catch my breath. "Look, I know I fucked up by not telling Beatrice about what was going on in my life. I explained everything to her. I admitted that I wanted to be with her regardless. I chose her, Blu."

"Get your foot out of my shop."

"What's going on? Tell me." I grind my molars, trying to keep control of my temper.

Tears hover in Blu's eyes, which she rapidly tries to blink away. Dread fills me. "Where is Beatrice?"

"Where is your *fiancée?*"

"Touché" is on the tip of my tongue. However, I tell her, "She had a boy last night. The father was there with her."

Blu's eyes widen.

"Yasmin admitted to making everything up concerning me and what we did. I've never touched that woman."

"Oh! You did tell Bea the truth?"

"Damn straight, I did. Where is she, Blu?"

My gut tells me something isn't right. The way Tracy reacted, and now Blu. Come to think of it, Zeke had been tight-lipped about Beatrice too.

"Tell me," I whisper. "Is she okay?"

"No." Blu lets out a shuddering breath. "She's in the hospital."

"What?" I hiss, thinking I've misheard. "I don't... Why?"

"I promised her I wouldn't tell you. I won't break that promise." She swallows. "She doesn't want to talk to you either." She reaches out and touches my hand, giving it a quick squeeze. "Give her time,

Ryker." Pulling herself together, she adds, "I have customers waiting."

She gently pushes me out of her store, and I drop to the bench on the sidewalk.

*What the hell is going on?*

I sit staring into nothing. For how long, I don't know. Nothing is making sense. Jared pulls up in front of me. The window goes down and he says, "Get in."

"I'm not sure that's a good idea."

"Get in, Ryker," Jared says, his voice leaving no room for argument.

I do as he says.

"Emma is going to kill me for this, so you better make it right before she finds out."

Watching him, I ask with dread, "Make what right?"

He sighs. "Beatrice had a miscarriage yesterday."

My ears ring as his words reach me.

I groan. "While I was there with one woman having someone else's baby, the woman I love was losing...*ours*... Oh God!"

I put my face in my hands and cry.

## 17

### BEATRICE

Through the night, I'd had trouble sleeping and my mind wouldn't stop spinning. I feel empty and upset. Finding out I was pregnant while simultaneously finding out I'd lost the babies had been a shock. I'd felt a bit off now and again but being pregnant had never crossed my mind. I'd felt numb more than anything.

Now I'm upset over not being pregnant with Ryker's children. The moment I'd found out what had happened, I knew that was what I wanted. Being a mom hadn't even been a thought until yesterday. And of all days, it had been the very one where that woman was in labor.

Just my luck of late.

No matter what I'd said to Blu last night, I don't

blame Ryker for anything that happened. My miscarriage would have occurred regardless. That's one thing the doctor emphasized.

I can't explain why I hurt so much over Ryker's choice to help the woman. It is ridiculous of me because he could be the baby's father. So why wouldn't he want to be there?

Lying in the hospital with nothing to do but think, my anger has drained away and I'm left crying for Ryker. I want him with me. Holding my hand. Telling me we would try again. Telling me he is with me.

He had asked me to wait for him. I had. I am.

Desperately needing him, I'm more than aware that Yasmin could still be in labor somewhere in the hospital.

It hurts.

I am jealous.

There are no more tears to fall after I've given myself a headache. The nurses are friendly to me and have kept the lights dimmed, which helps.

Curled on my side, my back to the door, I don't bother looking when I hear the door open and softly click shut. I want to wallow in self-pity.

Someone sits down heavily in the visitor's chair and I try to figure out who without looking. A few minutes pass, then I hear sniffling as though the person is crying.

The sound is masculine.

I roll to my back and stare in disbelief.

Ryker fills the chair, his head bowed and his shoulders shake. There is no mistaking his anguish.

"Ryker," I whisper, "come closer."

*I'm in love with this man.*

He shakes his head. "I deserve everything."

I start crying. "No, you don't. *Please* come to me." I hold my arms out to him and he moves.

He takes his shoes off, slides the side of the bed down, and then he scoots onto the bed and pulls me into his arms. I'm more than aware we have things to discuss. But right now, I just need him to hold me like this. Like he cares.

"I'm sorry, Beatrice," he whispers into my ear. "I'm so fucking sorry for everything." He nuzzles into my neck and continues, "No matter what you think of me or believe, I need you to know that I love you. I love you."

Slowly pulling back, his arms not releasing me, he says, "All these weeks, I would have been with you if I hadn't fucked up in the first place by omitting the truth. I never wanted to be with her. I only supported her here until I knew for sure." Tears fall down his face. "If I'd known what was happening to you yesterday, I would have been here with you, regardless of what else was going on. I would have chosen to be with you. It's easy for me to say that now, but with God as my witness, I mean every damn word."

I search his gaze and settle back into the bed, in his arms. He settles around me; his lips keep grazing the top of my head in a kiss.

"What happened with her?"

He audibly swallows, and says, "The father of her baby arrived while she was in labor. I couldn't get out of there fast enough. I'd bumped into Jared on my way to the exit, but he wouldn't tell me why he was there other than Emma was visiting a friend. I left the hospital and ended up outside your cottage. However, I'd decided I would wait until morning to start wooing you back into my life. Jared took pity on me an hour ago and told me what had happened."

After a pause, he says, "I still can't get over the fact that she thought nothing about setting me up. I mean, the baby is dark-skinned, as is his father. I don't know what Yasmin was thinking."

"I'm sorry she did that to you."

"It's over now. I'm coming to you with nothing between us except my heart."

Tears leak free as I whisper, "No one knows I was pregnant with twins. I didn't even know I was pregnant until I lost them." I inhale, and continue, "They were growing in my fallopian tube. It was close to rupturing, which is why I was in so much pain considering I was only a few weeks pregnant."

"God." He shudders and holds me. I'm nearly asleep when he says, "Can we start over, Beatrice? I want to woo you as a beautiful woman should be wooed by the man who loves her. But I want there to be no mistake. I've only wanted you from the moment we met. I'm playing for keeps, honey, if you'll have me."

"You've always had me," I whisper.

Perhaps there is something wrong with me for saying yes quickly, but I can't figure out what. I love him. I have no intention of saying those words yet because he does have to work for them.

## 18

### RYKER

As I drive up the road to the ranch I called home for the first twenty-one years of my life, I can't decide who is more nervous—Beatrice or me.

My parents know the whole mess I'd gotten myself into months ago. Dad had laughed and said only his son could get himself into such a mess. Mom had been another matter altogether. She'd yelled and cursed, and for the rest of my life, only Mom, God, and I would know exactly what she had said. Beatrice had told me she liked my mom already. Didn't surprise me.

It's spring now and the flowers Dad plants for Mom each year are in full bloom. Beatrice gasps as the house comes into view. "You grew up here?"

"Hmm," I mumble, spotting Mom and Dad on the porch.

"Mom is going to fuss over you like a daughter. I hope you're ready for that. I'm the big bad wolf in her books right now."

"I told you I liked your mom."

"You know how unfair that is?" I grumble.

She grins and, reaching over, kisses my cheek. "Stop being a big baby." She smirks. "I'm sure we can come up with a way to be very naughty when the lights go out."

I'm left blinking after her as she climbs from the truck and heads toward my parents. I will my body to behave and follow her, but at a slower pace. I love watching her. Her face is a delight and filled with happiness as my mom hugs her.

Mom takes her inside, passing me a grin over her shoulder as she does. Dad waits for me, a wince on his face.

"Mom wanted you to have words with me?"

"Yes." He laughs and tugs me into his arms. "I'm not going to because it looks like you've sorted yourself out." He squeezes tight and, keeping hold of my shoulders, says, "I wish you'd have come to us, Son. You know your mother; she'd have had the truth out of that woman months ago."

"Funny, you should say that; I told Levi the same thing."

He nods. "Valentina is annoyed you're visiting when she's at college, so be warned. Kennedy has decided she's going to check out Blossom Creek and is insisting on going back with you both."

"This is your fault for giving me sisters. Brothers wouldn't bother."

Dad snorts. "You believe that? Levi is there; Emma showed up and is now engaged to the sheriff. You went there and have planted roots with that woman of yours. How much do you want to bet that Kennedy won't come home either?" He glances at the house and adds, "And, how much do you want to bet if that happens, Valentina will follow? Do you know what that will mean? All your mother's babies thousands of miles away. She will have us selling and moving so fast my head will spin."

I laugh. "Well," I say, wrapping an arm around Dad's shoulders as we walk toward the door, "at least Mom will retire if you do that."

He pauses. "I hadn't thought about that." He grins. "That sounds like a good plan. Make sure you find good guys for your sisters."

*Unbelievable.*

We're still laughing as we enter the house.

Beatrice looks up from her position on the sofa and my heart flutters. She looks so happy. She's squished between Mom and Kennedy, and I can't quite see what they're doing, and then I do. Beatrice holds the picture of me at my graduation. I hate that picture.

I wink and move through into the kitchen with Dad. He sorts the coffee jug out while I go straight to the baked goods I know will be waiting and fill a plate.

It's good to be home.

## 19

## BEATRICE

THE ROOM IS PITCH BLACK AS I SLIP INTO BED BESIDE Ryker. For a month after I'd gotten out of the hospital, we had dated and shared heated kisses that left us both frustrated. Then, once we had taken our relationship further, we hadn't been able to resist each other. After two months of crazy sex between us, I'd asked him to move in with me. It was pointless him paying for a room at the inn when he spent most nights with me.

We've been inseparable since, so it is with incredible frustration that he has banned any kind of sex under his parents' roof.

I never agreed.

"I can feel the wheels turning in that head of yours," Ryker says.

"I'm thinking about your penis in my mouth," I reply with a grin on my face. Not that he can see it, but I enjoy teasing him.

He makes a gurgling noise.

"I'm wet thinking about it," I continue. "The way your cock twitches when I slide my tongue along the length and catch the drip of precum from the tip. You taste excellent, Ryker," I drawl.

My eyes have now become adjusted to the darkness and I see his erection tenting the covers. I hold in a dirty laugh.

"Would you like me to show you?"

"No," he hisses.

I roll to my side and offer him a wicked grin. I take his hand and press it to a naked breast. Ryker groans and arches his hips.

"I think your cock needs my mouth on it. Don't you want me to suck your cock, Ryker?" I whisper into his ear and bite the lobe.

"You are going to pay for this," he whispers, his hips once again arching.

I yank the covers from us and blink at how hard he is.

"Yummy." I giggle and quickly get between his legs.

"Beatrice," he growls in warning.

My mouth hovers over the wet tip as I say, "Yes, Ryker?" Then I stick my tongue out and swirl it around the head of his heavily swollen dick.

His hands grip the bedding beside him, and I go for more. My mouth opens and slides down the silky length as far as it will fit. I close my lips and hold him inside, my tongue doing wicked things. Ryker's legs tremble, and I swallow hard to get him more worked up.

His hands slide through my hair and hold my head in place as I continue to play and massage him. Ryker is slowly losing control.

I slip my hands beneath him and squeeze his ass cheeks, holding him still as he tries to move. I feel the lust sweeping through him, and it makes me feel powerful that I do this to him.

"Together," he hisses and quickly reaches for me.

We're on our sides with his face wedged between my legs, his mouth on my pussy. My eyes are focused on his erection and swollen balls.

I wrap my hand around the girth and guide him to my lips. I moan as his tongue wiggles between my sensitive folds, and I take him deep down my throat.

We haven't done this together before and I find it erotic. My breasts tingle as they press into his hips. When I move my hand to his balls and massage,

Ryker spikes his tongue into me. It feels like he's everywhere at once and I can't take anymore. I come hard, moaning around his dick, and I end up sucking and swallowing every drop of release from him.

"Fuck me!" he hisses, pulling me from him. He turns me around and cuddles me close.

"I should have known better than to tell you no sex," he comments with a soft smile on his lips.

"I love you," is my reply.

Ryker catches his breath, and tears glisten in his eyes. I haven't said those words to him before now.

I lean forward and brush his tears away with my lips. "I love you so much, Ryker. I loved you the night we first had sex. I never stopped. It's only grown." I wrap him close. "I didn't want you to think I was only saying those words because you said them to me. I wanted my words to mean as much to you as yours do to me."

"God, Beatrice. After that, it's killing me not saying them, but I'm going to show you how much I love you." He smirks, then kisses my nose. "As long as you promise to be quiet."

And love me he does.

Slowly.

Deeply.

Tenderly.

## 20

## EPILOGUE – LEVI DE LA FUENTE

VIVIEN IS WITH EMMA IN THE TAVERN OF ALL PLACES, and I'd promised my woman that I wouldn't interrupt.

However, after my conversation with Jared, I feel that interrupting is the thing to do.

Teagan scowls at me the moment I enter. "What?" I ask, thinking back to if I've pissed her off recently.

"I was told not to let you in."

"That makes no sense."

"It does when your sister and fiancée are looking through lots of online brochures of wedding dresses."

"Oh!" The bell goes off. "Can you please ask them to hide everything and that I need to talk to them. It can't wait. No one is hurt or dead."

Teagan rolls her eyes and disappears. A few minutes later, she waves me toward the booth where the girls are sitting.

Vivien jumps up and kisses me. "What is it?"

"I thought it was a good idea to come here at the time; now I'm not so sure."

"Levi," Emma snaps, "you're not making any sense. You've interrupted our girls' evening, so spill. Now!"

Vivien smiles.

I wish I'd thought about this first.

*Just get it out.*

"Jared called me, so I went into the station and talked to him. You know the, um, girl from that time you found me on the bed."

Emma snorts. "Naked and tied to the bed. Yes, I'm sure Vivien remembers, as do I."

Ignoring Emma, I hold Vivien's gaze. "The girl has been arrested in Boston for doing the same thing to four other guys." I sigh. "She did drug me. She usually robs the men too. But I had nothing in the apartment worth anything. My laptop and wallet had been in the office at Emelia's that night. My drinks here were on my tab. She got nothing," I say. "It's a relief to know what happened."

Vivien hugs me tight and whispers, "Maybe I'll let you tie me to the bed tonight." She nibbles on my earlobe and I go rock hard.

"Not fair."

She chuckles, and the sound goes straight to my balls. Vivien's chuckle always sounds thick and dirty. I'm going to have to ban her from making that sound in public.

Patting me on each cheek, she says, "Zeke is over there drinking all alone. Why don't you join him?"

"I can take the hint."

Emma snorts. "That wasn't a hint."

I narrow my gaze on my sister and Vivien pushes me toward the bar. "Be a good boy and we'll play later." She smacks me on the ass and I quickly sit at the bar before I become an embarrassment. I've left a barstool between Zeke and me.

The man is always quiet and doesn't say much. He's usually with Ryker in the back playing pool.

"Crashing your girl's night, so not cool," he says, grinning.

"They both should be used to me by now."

I indicate a bottle of water when Travis points at the Jack Daniels. "Working," I admit.

"On a break, then?" Zeke asks.

"Yeah," I say. "Any luck at finding someone for the office?"

Zeke has been interviewing for the office manager's job at the station. It's part-time, and I know from Bea and Ryker that he's had enough of the women who have been applying, or rather drooling over him.

"I don't get it," he mutters. "Why waste their time and mine?"

I snicker and say, "Why don't you ask Kennedy?"

"Who?" He frowns.

"Ryker's sister. She's coming back with them to stay for the summer." I shrug. "She knows her way around a computer. She also works at the firehouse in Great Falls on the weekends. In the office." I pause. "She's also adamant that she isn't getting married until she's in her late thirties. She's currently twenty-three."

Zeke stares at me, grabs my face, and slaps a kiss to my forehead. Now I'm the one staring. He laughs. "You should see your face right now." He tosses money on the bar. "I'm going to text Ryker to get his email address, then have him get the application to his sister."

He runs out the door.

"Okay, then." I fiddle with my ballcap, wave at my sister and my woman, and go back to work.

The End

I hope you enjoyed *A Rake in Blossom Creek* and look forward to book three of the series, *Heatwave in Blossom Creek*.

Thank you for reading *A Rake in Blossom Creek,* and thank you for your reviews! It's really appreciated.

Subscribe with your email to be alerted about new releases, sales, and events.
http://ronajameson.com

# HEATWAVE IN BLOSSOM CREEK

21ST JUNE 2021

Kennedy De La Fuente is enjoying life in Blossom Creek. It's the first time away from home, and the small apartment in the converted barn is perfect. The scenery is, for the most part, similar to that of Montana. The scenery at the small fire station, on the other hand, is nothing like it is back home. Her gaze has a mind of its own and is drawn to the handsome fire chief. Kennedy is finding it increasingly difficult to hide her feelings for the man. It's the very last thing she wants.

A heatwave is currently engulfing Blossom Creek and its inhabitants. The fire department is kept busy responding to medical emergencies and attempting to keep the forest surrounding the town from burning. Zeke Davidson has begun to prefer being out on a job so that he's not in close quarters with his office manager, who wears very little due to the oppressive heat. The woman is a distraction he doesn't need—in fact, she is the very last thing he wants.

Once again, the Between the Sheets Book Club is more interested in gossip than a book. This time, the ladies are discussing Zeke and Kennedy.

## MY BROTHER'S GIRL
BAD BOY ROCKERS, BOOK 1

Thalia jumps at the chance to spend the summer with her new 'boyfriend' and his family in Alabama. It means she gets to have fun with Liam instead of heading home to her restrictive life. What she hasn't bargained for, is Liam's older brother, Jack—her life suddenly becomes complicated.

Jack gives her sultry glances and touches her heart in a way no one ever has while Liam acts indifferent. No matter what happens this summer, she has to remember to stay away from Jack—however, that becomes impossible when he's everywhere she is.

What is a girl to do?

He has muscle.

He has tattoos.

He has piercings.

He has a mouth that makes her panties wet.

He's her boyfriend's older brother.

Available at all online retailers.

# LOVE IN PURGATORY
## DE LA FUENTE SERIES, BOOK 2

*Forgive me father for I have sinned . . .*

Dante De La Fuente, the oldest of his siblings, is a man of the cloth—bound by honor and sacred vows to serve the church. But untold truths and misconceptions are what led him down his religious path. After the death of his mother, his trust in his father was quickly shattered. Decades later, Dante finds himself in turmoil, questioning his faith, and possibly his sanity.

*And lead us not into temptation . . .*

Emelia, and her twin brother, Diego, are the youngest of the De La Fuente siblings. For years, Emelia's been carrying the burden of knowing the truth surrounding her and Diego's birth. Exposing the long held secret could break their family apart; keeping it to herself could destroy her and Dante both. She holds the key to setting Dante free of his torment

...and getting what her heart desires most.

*. . . and the truth will set you free*

# OTHER BOOKS BY AUTHOR

## NEW SERIES - Boston Bay Vikings

*Book 1: Camden: on the ice*

*Book 2: Bennett: on the ice*

*Book 3: Ethan: on the ice*

## NEW SERIES - Blossom Creek

*Book 1: Christmas at Emelia's*

*Book 2: A Rake in Blossom Creek*

*Book 3: Heatwave in Blossom Creek*

*Book 4: Secret Love in Blossom Creek*

*Book 5: Mischief in Blossom Creek*

## Bad Boy Rockers

*Book 1: My Brother's Girl (Sizzle) (Jack 'Jack' & Thalia)*

*Book 2: Past Sins (Spicy) (Reece & Callie)*

*Book 3: My Best Friend's Sister (Sultry) (Donovan & Mara)*

*Book 4: Never Let Go (Savor) (Ryder & Dahlia)*

*Book 5: Saving Jace (Sinful) (Jace & Savannah)*

*Book 6: Silent Night (Novella)*

## Kincaid Sisters

*Book 1: Meant to be Mine*

*Book 2: You Were Always Mine*

*Book 3: Will You be Mine*

## McKenzie Brothers

*Book 1: Seduce (Michael & Lily)*

*Book 1.5: The Wedding (Novella)*

*Book 2: Rapture (Sebastian & Carla)*

*Book 3: Delight (Ruben & Rosie)*

*Book 4: Entice (Lucien & Sabrina)*

*Book 5: Cherished (Ramon & Noah)*

*Book 5.5: A McKenzie Christmas (Novella)*

## De La Fuente Family (McKenzie Spinoff)

*Book 1: Love in Montana (Sylvia & Eric)*

*Book 2: Love in Purgatory (Dante & Emelia)*

*Book 3: Love in Bloom (Mateo & Erin)*

*Book 4: Love in Country (Aiden & Sarah)*

*Book 5: Love in Flame (Diego & Rae)*

*Book 6: Love in Game (Kasey & Felicity)*

*Book 7: Love in Education (Andie & Seth)*

## McKenzie Cousins

## (McKenzie Spinoff)

*Book 1: Baby Makes Three (Sirena & Garrett)*

*Book 2: A Business Decision (Michael & Brooke)*

**Holiday Season**

*Kissing Under the Mistletoe*

*A Soldier's Christmas*

*Jingle Bells*

**Written as Rona Jameson**

*Butterfly Girl*

*Come Back to Me*

*Summer at Rose Cottage*

*Tears in the Rain*

*Twenty Eight Days*

# ACKNOWLEDGEMENTS

Editors: Nadine Winningham

Proofreaders: Nadine Winningham and Lynne Garlick

# ABOUT THE AUTHOR

Alison, who was born in England, writes romance and erotic romance as Lexi Buchanan. Under the name Rona Jameson she writes contemporary and young adult/coming of age romance, and romantic suspense. She moved to Ireland with her husband, four children, a dog, and a cat in 2010.

*Follow on social media:*

Website: http://ronajameson.com
Email: authorlexibuchanan@gmail.com

facebook.com/lexibuchananauthor
twitter.com/AuthorLexi
instagram.com/authorlexib
bookbub.com/author/lexi-buchanan
pinterest.com/authorlexi
amazon.com/Lexi-Buchanan/e/B009SPA94U

Printed in Great Britain
by Amazon

74543566R10098